BLOODY TRAIL TO DORADO

Who took a knife to Sam Brennan and left him to die in his barn at Dorado? Who spent twelve months robbing the Union Pacific Railroad? Brennan's sons, Luke and Sean, were arrested for both crimes when they rode down from the Bighorns with fresh blood on their hands. Hours away from the hangman's noose, they were broken out of jail by wily Fess La Lone. With a crooked lawman, a US marshal and a mysterious sniper all to be faced, Luke's life was on the line. Could he survive?

JIM LAWLESS

BLOODY TRAIL TO DORADO

Complete and Unabridged

LINFORD
Leicester

First published in Great Britain in 2002 by
Robert Hale Limited
London

First Linford Edition
published 2003
by arrangement with
Robert Hale Limited
London

British Library CIP Data

Lawless, Jim
    Bloody trail to Dorado.—Large print ed.—
Linford western library
    1. Western stories
    2. Large type books
    I. Title
    823.9′14 [F]

ISBN 0–7089–4863–4

Published by
F. A. Thorpe (Publishing)
Anstey, Leicestershire

Set by Words & Graphics Ltd.
Anstey, Leicestershire
Printed and bound in Great Britain by
T. J. International Ltd., Padstow, Cornwall

This book is printed on acid-free paper

Part One

First Blood

1

They came across the deer when the skies were reddening in the West and the Sioux were so close Sean swore he could smell their stink, the horses snorting and shying nervously and Luke cursing because the last thing they wanted was sudden noise to bring those red devils howling down out of the Bighorns and crawling all over them. But they couldn't pass. The doe with one foreleg caught in a rusty iron trap was panting in the coarse grass, soulful dark eyes silently pleading with them to set it free or put it out of its misery. It would have taken a cold-blooded bastard to turn around and ride away.

'A shot'll be like offerin' honey to a family of bears,' Luke said, as he swung out of the saddle. 'Throw me your knife.'

Sean packed a Bowie. He slipped it out of his boot, Luke caught it by the hilt, and one clean sweep of the razor-sharp blade opened the trapped animal's throat. The heart pumped strongly for several seconds. Then death came, leaving the doe mercifully free from pain and Luke's arm and shirt front soaked in bright blood. Unusually disturbed, he kicked about in the scrub, came up with enough mossy rocks to pile in a clattering heap on the dead animal and the rusty iron clamp that had caused it agony for perhaps two long days. When he straightened, dusty, sweating, with the deer's blood already stiffening on his skin and clothes, it was to see his brother, still mounted, shaking his dark head.

'You're too damn soft-hearted for your own good,' Sean said quietly, but there was affection in his voice and maybe that and lingering memories of what they'd been through distracted him because he made a poor job of cleaning the knife before tucking it into his boot.

Luke was to remember that, later.

After another hour they were out of the tall timber and heading down through the foothills with the Powder River glinting in the distance. By that time, Sean's sorrel was obviously lame, and for a time the rangy young man walked awkwardly alongside it, lean fist clamped on the bridle close to the bit, every so often stopping to give the horse's hind fetlock a rub — and that 'every so often' got to be more and more frequent.

'He'll take your weight,' Luke said after a while, 'if we go real easy.'

'I confess I'm too damn tired to think, never mind walk.' Sean patted the sorrel's neck apologetically, swung lightly into the saddle and squinted across his right shoulder at the crimson skies. 'How much further?'

Luke chuckled. His throat was dry, his half-full canteen was in his saddle-bag — but he was leaving it there, forcing himself to wait, letting the thirst build up inside him because a drink when they got home would be that much more welcome, and a drink shared with the father they hadn't seen for more than twelve months, well . . .

'Ten miles,' he said huskily, 'if I remember right — and, by God, I remember this part of Wyoming Territory like I never left on that crazy trip; like that whole time away was just one bad dream.'

'That close,' Sean said, almost inaudibly, and not for the first time Luke felt a twinge of conscience. He was six years older than his brother. Sean had been eighteen when they rode away from the home spread, his face pale beneath its tan when they stopped on that last rise and looked back towards the run-down buildings and corrals to wave to their pa. At that point he might have turned back, but a young man is stuffed full of enough bravado to smother sentiment and common sense. The moment had passed, but Luke knew the memory had remained like an image carved in rock.

They crossed Crazy Woman Creek at dusk, splashing out of the shallows and up the bank to lope through the cottonwoods and on towards the ridge that was bathed in red light, chasing their long shadows home. And on that ridge, using his lame horse as an excuse, Sean drew rein and gazed across the open grassland.

'You reckon he'll . . .?' he said huskily, then shook his head and broke off to slip from the saddle and stoop to tend to the sorrel's fetlock.

'What I reckon is, when we get there I'll be hard pressed to decide which one of you's the most pleased,' Luke said, and found himself unable to pull his eyes away from the distant buildings.

'He'll have no . . . no hard feelings?'

'We rode out because there was nothing left in the poke, the barn was fallin' down around us and the promise of salvation was beckoning from a long way away across some pretty tough

7

territory,' Luke said. 'OK, so it took us longer than we'd figured — '

'And we're comin' back empty handed — '

'Yeah,' Luke said ruefully, 'but Sam Brennan's two sons are comin' back, and that'll please him above all else.'

'I think you're right,' Sean said. Then, 'Yeah, you know, Luke, I'm sure of it,' and in his voice Luke detected the return of confidence, a gathering strength. The boy who had left home with his brother to make their fortunes and found the task beyond their combined capabilities was returning a grown man, and suddenly he was aware, and eager to show off.

'Mount up,' Luke said, smothering a grin. 'If he won't budge, then carry the goddamn horse. Over yonder is Dorado. We're home, Sean.'

2

They had expected silence, but as they clattered around the corral and crossed the yard towards the house it seemed that they were disturbing the silence of the dead. Glass windows Sam Brennan had always been so proud of reflected the last rays of the dying sun, but emitted no light because in the big main room no oil lamps were lit. Nor anywhere else. To their right, alongside the broad slope that eased down towards the barn, the heavy door of the long, low bunkhouse swung open on creaking hinges. On the slab of stone that served for a step, a battered, overturned bucket clanked forlornly as it rolled to the thin breeze.

Then a horse whinnied, and Sean said nervously, 'He's home, for sure, but I guess he didn't get your wire.'

'And nothing around here's changed,

except for the worse,' Luke said, but he was talking for the sake of it as his eyes ranged wide in the gathering gloom.

Wrong. Something was wrong. But what?

The lame sorrel blew softly and metal jingled as Sean stepped down. The bucket rolled noisily off the bunkhouse step and was held fast by a tangle of weeds. Weeds everywhere. Springing up in the yard, the corral. Tumbleweed climbing over itself against the splintered boards of the old barn. Dust thick on the ground, shaped by the wind but not by the passing of horses, or men.

'More than a year,' Luke said quietly, 'and the only way Pa's gone is downhill.'

'He was old, and tired,' Sean said. He flicked the reins around the rail, fashioned a hitch, looked towards the house. 'A lonely old man, so what was left for him when we rode out?'

'Hope.' Luke's voice was tight. He didn't like the emptiness: the oppressive quiet that lay thick and ominous under the sighing of the night breeze; the gaping bunkhouse door that told him men had ridden away and the one that remained no longer cared.

Doors, he corrected. Because the house door was also open, a black hole at the back of the wide gallery — and that, too, was wrong.

'Sam!' Luke called. 'Sam Brennan!'

His own voice came back to him, flattened and thinned by its wasted flight, and Sean laughed uneasily.

'He was also hard of hearin'. We'd best go inside.'

Luke grunted. He slid from the saddle, hitched his horse alongside the sorrel and made for the steps.

Sean was hanging back.

'You think it's OK?'

'Like you said, there's one way to find out.'

But the house, when they stepped over the threshold, was cold and empty.

Familiar smells brought an ache to Luke's throat. He saw Sean pick up his pa's hat from a chair, absently slap it against his thigh so that dust drifted in the gloom. The youngster was frowning as he looked around at the dark furniture, the bare floorboards, the tintypes on the walls and the rack of shiny long rifles and pistols kept lovingly oiled by the old man. The only time he'd seen his pa without that hat was when he was in bed. And when he was in bed the hat would be alongside him, within easy reach, shapeless as ever but cocked jauntily on top of his stovepipe boots.

'Not in the house,' Sean said in a voice more suited to a church, and Luke nodded.

'But here. I feel it. I know it. That hat's a part of him.'

'You reckon that was his horse we heard?'

Luke took a breath. 'Maybe — but it was his habit to let it run loose in the corral.'

'Maybe his habits went out the window when we left.'

'Maybe. But I've got me a bad feeling . . . '

He crossed to a familiar dark corner, found the familiar brown jug, poked a finger through the handle and lifted it to draw the cork with his teeth. He rested the jug on his bent elbow, raised his arm and took a quick drink, gasped as the raw spirit hit his dry throat like lye poured into an open wound.

'Here — '

'No, Luke — '

'Take it,' Luke said, and watched as his brother drank, saw the tears flood his eyes and knew that their pa's moonshine whisky was only partly to blame.

The house didn't run to a kitchen, or a back door. They retraced their steps, clattered across the gallery and down the steps and Luke led the way down the shallow slope towards the barn. On the way they passed close to the bunkhouse. Even without stepping inside they could smell the mustiness. A filthy cloth hung limp from a nail under the shelf where men had shaved, but that had been a long time ago. A thin cake of soap had dried out and cracked; a broken mirror lay in the weeds alongside the bucket once used to carry water, and the oft trodden path that led from bunkhouse to barn was now overgrown.

The smell when they walked into the barn was so strong they could taste it, and the hairs on Luke's neck prickled as he quickly stepped to one side away from the door and peered into the gloom. Instinctively, his hand had dropped to the butt of his sixgun. Sean was across at their old buckboard and swearing softly and repeatedly under his breath. Somewhere a cooling board creaked. And through the cracks in the west wall the sinking sun cast rays of light across the straw-strewn dust that were like long fingers of blood.

Blood! Luke spat the coppery taste out of his mouth and dragged the back of his hand across his wet lips, and was left with nothing but the taste of despair.

'That him?' Sean croaked.

'Quiet!'

The fading light's blood-red fingers reached out to the crumpled figure lying up against one wheel of the buckboard, touched it, and left their stain. But when Luke drew near, he saw that beneath that colourful illusion of blood there was the ugliness of crusted reality, streaks that ran into the old man's sightless eyes from his ripped, naked scalp, ugly stab wounds visible through the ripped shirt, the slashed flesh of forearms and clawed hands that had been raised as a last, futile defence.

Beneath a stubble of grey whiskers, the scrawny throat had been slashed from ear to ear.

At his shoulder, Sean gagged.

'Jesus!' he gasped. 'We should never 've left him — '

'Stand still, get your hands clear of your guns!'

The voice came roaring out of the

shadows deep inside the barn, shocking, sending them staggering with its power. As Luke whirled, saw nothing but the glint of steel, behind him another voice raged, 'Do as the man says, lift your hands high, or die!'

And then, as Sean whimpered in fright and backed clumsily into Luke as he straightened from the fighting crouch he had instinctively adopted, a man strutted from the rear of the barn and approached Sam Brennan's body, eyes glittering, pistol jutting from a big fist, a badge shining on his vest.

'Yeah, this is the law, fellers, you've had a barrel of fun, but all that rampagin' you've enjoyed in the past twelve months ends right here, right now.'

'Nah,' the other man said. 'They get tried, then they hang — that's where it ends.'

'I like it,' the lawman said, lazily stirring the dead man with the toe of his boot and drawing a fearsome growl of anger from Luke. 'They do us a big favour, then hang. Hell, Zak, that's pure, untarnished, poetic justice.'

Another lean man emerged from the side shadows, then another, powerful, unshaven, sixguns glinting. That made four in all, and Luke recognized the late arrivals: a bronc-buster name of Lannigan; a saloon swamper called Stilson who hung around begging for drinks when he wasn't cleaning out the livery stables.

And he wondered who else was there, in the barn, as he listened to the rustle of straw overhead, flicked a glance up at the board floor of the hay-loft, saw a strand drift down and a movement between the badly fitting boards . . .

Luke lowered his eyes to meet the cold grey eyes of badge-toting Marshal Cleaver Magg who, he recalled, had been a lowly town constable collecting fines and chasing stray dogs when they left, and said, 'What do you mean, we do you a big favour?'

'Killin' your old man saved us a job. You want to take on your brother, make it two out of three?'

'You know we didn't kill him,' Sean said hoarsely.

'No, boy,' Magg said, 'that ain't what I know. I look at your brother's shirt, and what I see is fresh blood — '

'We found a trapped deer,' Sean said. 'Luke took pity on it, slashed its throat.'

'So how come you got dry blood on your hands?'

Luke flashed a warning glance — but it was too late.

'It was my knife he used. I . . . ' Sean said, and trailed off into silence as he saw Magg's savage grin and realized his mistake.

'Allus did tote a knife when you was a kid,' Magg said. 'In your right boot, as I recall,' and he nodded to Lannigan and Stilson.

The two men swaggered forward. Lannigan, the bronc-buster, grabbed a shoulder and rammed his pistol into Sean's face so hard the muzzle rattled against his teeth and the foresight split his lip, spilling yet more bright blood.

Stilson dropped to one knee, one big hand reached out to clamp on Sean's dusty boot — and in Luke's head a pulse of memory began to hammer and he was back in the woods watching the wet knife being tucked away.

The hilt and blade of the big Bowie the gunman pulled free were a rusty red before it was lifted high to catch the dying light and, as Stilson rose and turned away, there was a matching, fiendish light of triumph dancing in Cleaver Magg's eyes.

'Goddamn,' he said softly, 'he kills his pa and cares so little he don't bother to wipe the knife clean — '

'A deer!' Sean yelled, blood dribbling from his chin as he pulled away from Lannigan's pistol. 'Christ, I already told you — '

'No!' Cleaver Magg roared. He strode forward, stood spread-legged, thrust his face at Sean. 'Your own words, sonny: *'Jesus, we should never've left him'*. What you did was, you murdered your old man for some damn reason, then rode out a-ways because the job was done and you could take time over a drink with your thieving brother before comin' back for the money. You didn't figure on nobody ridin' in, findin' the old man bleedin' like a stuck pig.'

'We left him twelve months ago, ain't been back till now,' Luke said quietly.

'I already smelled strong drink on your breath.'

'We took a drink in the house, if you were watching, you know that,' Luke said, and shook his head. 'Somebody killed him — Indians, renegades — but it wasn't us.'

'Yeah,' Magg said. 'Tell that to the judge.'

'You're not making sense. You talk about a twelve month rampage, us killing Pa then coming back for the money. What money, Magg? What the hell's going on?'

'The cash you stole from the trains you robbed,' Zak Theaker said. He came out of the shadows to join Magg, Winchester in the crook of his arm. 'Christ, it has to be stashed somewhere,

20

you've been too busy stealin' to spend.'

'Stealing?' Sean said, flabbergasted. 'We spent a whole year breaking our backs digging for gold — then had the lot stole from us.'

'Pity,' Magg said, winking at Theaker. 'All that time and nothing to show us 'cept a bloody knife.'

He turned, snapped his fingers, and Art Stilson passed him the big Bowie. Magg whipped off his bandanna, wrapped it around the bloody weapon, thrust it into the waistband of his pants.

'Evidence,' he said, and Theaker laughed.

'For the last time,' Luke said, 'we didn't kill him.'

'Aw, who the hell cares.' Magg turned aside and spat contemptuously, narrowly missing the dead man's boot. 'I already said you done us a favour. You'll hang, of that there ain't no doubt — but when the two of you get your necks stretched it won't be for Sam Brennan, it'll be for that unarmed train driver your kid brother damn near cut in half with his shotgun.'

21

3

After two hours' hard riding they splashed through the Powder River, sending up sheets of fine spray that sparkled in the light of the rising moon, then pushed on due south towards the town of Linch with Magg and Theaker some way out in front, Lannigan and Stilson taking up the rear. If Luke had any notion of making a break, it had been blocked at the outset when Magg ordered the brothers' ankles roped together under their horses' bellies and their wrists lashed to the horn. The bindings he used were wet rawhide. As if that wasn't enough, he then linked the horses by a lass-rope hitched to their saddle-horns that from time to time during the long ride snapped cruelly tight.

From the start, after Magg had checked the rawhide bindings and issued the order to move out, the only sounds were the drum of hooves on baked earth, the blowing of the horses, the creaking of leather and the occasional distant cry of a coyote. But Luke Brennan heard none of these for he was a man riding in a nightmare, a man torn apart by the agony of his regrets. And the agony was made worse by the sure knowledge that there was no going back, that nothing could be changed.

As the wet rawhide dried and tightened around his wrists he was tortured by the memory of his father's forlorn figure growing ever smaller and more indistinct on the edge of the yard as they trailed dust away from the home spread; tortured by the inescapable fact that the theft of their gold — in a brutal attack that had left Sean with a broken arm — had made their year-long efforts to raise a sizeable grubstake a complete waste of time.

Yet even if they had returned with a small fortune, would it have been of any consequence? The man whose memory

23

had been their driving force throughout those twelve months was dead, buried by his two grieving sons less than an hour ago behind the spread he could no longer manage. The money they had worked for, and lost, had been for him, not them.

Now, they stood accused of his murder. And it occurred to Luke as, in his torment, he lifted his eyes to the cold clear moon, that the reason why Sam Brennan had died and Cleaver Magg and his cohorts were lurking in the barn's shadows on the very night they returned from their travels was a question that should have been asked at once, must still be asked while there was still time. A good lawyer would worry that point like a dog at a bone, chipping away with questions like a hardrock miner's pick until . . .

Here Luke sighed deeply, for they had no money to finance a defence and in Linch — unless a lot had changed — there was but one lawyer, and he a slick-haired shyster named Reuben Flint who gazed on the world with shifty eyes from the comfortable pockets of rich cattlemen.

That lofty position was something Sam Brennan had never got close to achieving; he had never been anything more than a squatter on the land he had named Dorado. It could be said that his death had removed a festering sore from the range, but for the sons who had murdered him there would be no compassion.

They had one true friend, and it was with the stirring of a faint hope that Luke recalled Fess La Lone, a man who spent most of the year hunting with an old Sharps .50 up in the Bighorns but came down through the canyons and arroyos when he had skins to sell or — and this was the hope — when the mood took him.

La Lone was footloose, a drifter, a man who would stay in one place while he could scratch a living, move on to new territory when the game began outguessing him and the pickings were thin. But he was single-minded, bloody-minded, saw the world in black and white and would ride fifty miles if he got wind of a fight.

And the way this business was shaping up it was likely, Luke reckoned, to become the grandaddy of all the bruising, battling encounters stringy old Fess La Lone had fought over the past fifty odd years.

Riding the trail into Linch on that moonlit night was hauntingly familiar, and more than once Luke saw Sean turning his head to look about him as they passed a bluff he recognized, or rounded a turn to reveal a twisting silver creek flanked by grey-green cottonwoods where, on trips into town for supplies, he had many times pulled the buckboard off the trail and stopped to enjoy a quiet smoke.

Linch was a small town, but as they left the Powder River far behind the land flattened to a broad plain and from some way off its lights became visible like fireflies caught in a spider's web.

Magg glanced back, then faced front and the pace picked up. They drew closer to the town, at first imperceptibly and then with a rush so that the naked plain quickly became dotted with the shacks of those who lived far out, then with larger buildings with white picket fences enclosing well-watered lawns.

One house loomed larger than the rest. Lights gleamed in curtained windows. A figure could be seen standing well back on a veranda. The tip of a cigar glowed.

At that point, Zak Theaker reined his horse back until the brothers drew level, then reached across to place a lighted cigarette between their lips. Sean shook his head, his eyes dull. Theaker shrugged, sent the cigarette sparking into the grass. Then he snapped open a clasp knife from his pocket, reached across to sever Luke's bindings and rode around to do the same for Sean.

Luke held the cigarette between numb fingers and, through teeth clenched against the pain of returning circulation, he said, 'Magg's orders? I guess it would look bad, us riding in like turkeys trussed for Christmas.'

'Let's just say Judge Flint don't allow anything to impede the natural course of justice.'

'*Judge* Flint?'

'On the veranda. Small-town lawyer grown fat. Likes everything done proper so there ain't no indignant squawks from the church-goin' ladies of the town.'

'And this natural course?'

'Commit the crime, get caught, pay the penalty.'

'My God!' Sean said distantly.

Theaker grinned. 'Yeah. A trial's no more than an unnecessary irritation.'

He swung away to rejoin Magg, in passing lifted a hand in casual salute to the shadowy figure on the veranda. Magg peeled off towards the picket fence, swung out of the saddle, and the white gate creaked as he opened it and approached the house.

The rest of them, like a troop of cavalry returning with prisoners and escort to home fort, continued on to ride into Linch at a spanking pace and draw rein in front of the ancient timber jail.

Five minutes later, their gunbelts taken from them and looped over a peg in the office, Luke and Sean Brennan were walked through to the rear of the jail where the doors of two adjoining strap-steel cells clanged shut on them and took away the last of their freedom.

* * *

'Luke?'

'Yeah.'

'In the barn that . . . that didn't look like Pa.'

'It wasn't. Pa had gone. What you saw was nothing.'

A cigarette glowed in the darkness. The harsh smoke drifted to Luke as he lay on the hard bunk, hands behind his head staring at . . . at nothing. Was that all they had to look forward to? Had there ever been a time when the Brennan clan's prospects looked bright? Their ma died at thirty, with Sean still in short pants. They made the long trek to Wyoming because for many years after his wife's death Sam Brennan had been quietly and stoically going bust. It got too much to bear. For him, they spent eighteen months working lodes around Alder Gulch that had petered out years before, headed east when they heard news of fresh strikes in the Black Hills of the Dakotas and lost what they scraped out of the earth in the next six months to fierce renegades who preyed on prospectors mentally and physically worn to a frazzle. And when they rode through the Bighorns into Wyoming to the spread on the south side of Crazy Woman Creek it was to be greeted by worse than nothing; by a situation worse than all their waking nightmares.

'Why were they there?' he whispered into the darkness. 'Hell, we're talkin' about a run-down spread forty, fifty miles north of Linch. The ride took them five hours. Why would Magg go there?'

'Looking for train robbers,' Sean said, and his laugh was bitter. 'Old Sam Brennan and his sons have been holdin' up trains, Luke.'

'They wouldn't ride on the off chance.'

The cot creaked as Sean stirred restlessly.

'Maybe they had evidence pointin' that way.'

'All right, but Sam was cut to ribbons. If they found him like that, found him dead, why hang around?'

'You heard Theaker. We stashed all that money we stole, walked in with them lookin' for it.'

Luke turned his head towards the next cell, saw the thin plume of cigarette smoke rising straight and white in the pale starlight, the long outline of his brother's spare frame stretched out beneath the threadbare blanket.

'You remember Fess La Lone?'

'Surely. Feisty old-timer. Used to show me his skinnin' knives, gave me that Bowie, called it a measly pig-sticker.' His head turned. 'Hell, Luke, you don't reckon — '

'No. No, that's not what I think.'

'Then what?'

In the darkness, Luke shook his head, and shrugged. 'I think,' he said, 'what we've been listenin' to is all truth, or all lies.'

'Then it's all lies, because we both know we spent a year away and came back to find Pa dead.'

'So who's lying?'

'Cleaver Magg?'

'Why?'

Again the cot creaked, this time startlingly loud in the darkness as Sean swung his legs over the side and sat up. The cigarette sparked, then went black as he dropped it on the dirt floor and crushed it beneath his boot.

'Because he was robbin' trains,' he said, and his voice throbbed with suppressed excitement. 'It's the only answer, Luke: Cleaver Magg is crooked.'

4

For Luke Brennan, the world he knew had gone and the one he had been dumped in with cruel haste was moving too fast.

He awoke at dawn and lay on the hard cot with the thin blanket covering him like a shroud, the air chill enough to stiffen the skin of his exposed face, his mind a whirl. It was as if he and Sean had ridden down from the mighty Bighorns to be swept up by a howling storm that showed no sign of abating. Torn apart by hardship that had seemed never-ending, they came home disconsolate but anticipating some relief and were caught up in a twister that had ripped away every vestige of their past and left their future in doubt.

The harsh reality of their situation was rammed home when, with the light streaming through the barred windows warmed by the rays of the rising sun, an inner door slammed open, keys jangled, and Cleaver Magg and a deputy built like a steer came down the passageway carrying steaming mugs and tin plates of food.

They delivered Luke's breakfast first, opening his cell door and dumping plate and mug on the floor hard enough to slop coffee and leave a crisp fried bacon rasher trailing in the dirt.

Then it was Sean's turn and, as soon as Luke saw his brother kicking the blanket aside and coming off the cot, he knew he'd been too deep in his own misery to think straight. It was clear that the boy had been simmering for most of the night. Now he was fired up, and he came off the cot and uncurled his long frame with his blazing eyes fixed on the marshal.

It was too late for a warning.

'Hey, Luke,' he called, as Magg sent his plate clattering across the floor and the deputy stepped inside to hand him the steaming mug, 'here's that crooked marshal goes out robbin' trains, like to get us hanged for — '

The reaction was instant, and violent.

Grunting with effort, the big deputy back-handed Sean with a stiff left arm and the meaty edge of a clenched fist. The blow crashed into his temple with the power of an axe biting into a tree. He staggered backwards, twisted to hit the edge of the bunk with the side of his knee and his legs crumpled.

As he went down, Magg stepped forward, growling, and elbowed the deputy aside. In the same movement he swung his right foot in a vicious kick. His boot sank into the pit of Sean's stomach.

'Leave him be!' Luke roared.

He sprang to the strap-steel bars between the cells, grabbed them with clawed fingers and shook until they rattled. The big deputy turned, looked at him impassively, then flung the mug across the cell.

The tin mug clanged against the bars. Scalding hot coffee sprayed

Luke's face and neck. Pain was a wave of intense agony searing sensitive nerve ends. Breath hissed through his teeth. Gasping, scrubbing a sleeve across his streaming face, he reeled backwards and sat down heavily on the cot. Through squinted eyes he had a blurred picture of Magg driving thumping kicks into Sean's body. One crashed into his shoulder. Another scraped across his face and Sean rolled, got his knees under him and spat out a bloody tooth.

But Magg wouldn't back off. Jaw muscles bunched, eyes ugly, he waited until Sean was up into an unsteady crouch, then swung a looping punch that took him on the cheekbone and drove him sprawling. The marshal's knees bent as he prepared to leap forward, and Luke's mind raced ahead so that he could see Magg launching himself to drop heavily with both knees on Sean's chest, hear the sickening crackle as ribs cracked beneath the weight . . .

Then the deputy had a hand clamped on Magg's shoulder.

'Enough,' he said, and pulled Magg away. 'The trial's at noon, they'll hang at dawn. You don't want to spoil the town's fun by beatin' this feller to death.'

'Noon?' Luke said, and felt the cold hand of despair clamp his heart as, slumped on hands and knees, his warm blood dripping into a thickening pool on the dirt floor, Sean looked at him with panic in his eyes. 'If I'm doing the defending, that doesn't give me much time to prepare a case.'

'You could do your preparin' for a whole damn year,' Magg said, 'but there'll still be witnesses'll swear they was there and recognized all three of you Brennans hold up the Union Pacific and gun down the guard.'

'Then they're lying.'

'Townsfolk? Men who trusted you and your kin before you took to a life of crime?'

'You know damn well we've been out

of the territory for more than twelve months.'

'I know you've been somewhere. But spreadin' talk of a damn fool trip out west is a handy way of explainin' why most of the time you were too busy to be where you should have been.'

'If you went out there with your suspicions, Pa must have told you. Are you saying he was lying?'

Magg shook his head, gestured to the deputy and they left the cell and locked the door. 'You still ain't listenin'. There's a spread out there on Crazy Woman Creek goin' by the fancy name Dorado but so run down if a man tried to raise goats they'd starve to death. It got that way not because you and your brother were off in the mountains scratchin' for gold dust, but because all three Brennans figured there was an easier way of gettin' rich.' Magg stared at Luke, thick finger poked out as he absently jiggled the big ring of keys on one forefinger. 'It's a plain fact that your pa was away nigh on as long as you two boys because most of the time all three of you were together. You were out there flaggin' down trains, tryin' your damnedest to make the James boys look like a couple of greenhorns.'

★ ★ ★

'There's worse to come,' Luke said.

Their plates had been wiped clean. Luke had drunk half his coffee, then passed the mug through the bars to give back to Sean what had been thrown across the cell to splash in his face. Talk had come and gone. Time had passed; in painful silence, several hours had crept by and the sun now slanted into both cells so that the air was stifling. Through the thin timber walls and glassless barred windows they had listened to the town awake, heard wagons roll, heard the drum of horses' hooves on the dusty street and the good-natured banter of cowboys from outlying ranches in for supplies; heard the shrill laughter of children and the rapid clatter of their feet on plankwalks as they headed for school.

Now, by Luke's reckoning, it was close to noon.

'I know,' Sean said, his voice a painful mumble. 'If Reuben Flint's made judge then he'll operate the same as he always did, only with more power.'

'I was thinkin' of the walk from here to the saloon.'

A match scraped as Sean lit a cigarette. Luke saw the flame tremble as it was applied, the hasty sideways glance from Sean, the quick jerk of the wrist that flicked the match into the corner.

'In what way? You think people will make as much of this trial as they can? Have fun at our expense?'

'If someone's been robbing the Union Pacific, there'll've been a shortage of money — maybe still is. If it's real bad, Foster over at the bank will have been forced to look hard at those businesses deep in debt, maybe foreclose.'

'Bad feelings.' Sean nodded, drew shakily on the cigarette. 'If people have gone bust they'll be out on street as soon's news gets around. You thinkin' . . . ' He stopped, stared fixedly at the end of his cigarette. 'You thinkin' of a lynch mob?'

'Lynching's a possibility,' Luke said, then caught Sean's sudden shudder and instantly regretted the words. He stood up, paced for a few silent moments, then sucked in a breath and shook his head. 'I don't know what I'm thinking. Maybe I should keep my mouth shut, not make things worse — '

'Could they be?' Sean laughed nervously, and when he looked up his eyes were unnaturally bright. 'You never noticed, but when Magg brought us in, he dumped my Bowie on the desk. On the way through — '

'You picked it up?'

'Damn right. It's in my boot, so if things get real tough . . . '

'Well, we're not dead yet,' Luke said. 'Trouble is, I can't figure Magg. The man could be genuine, he's a lawman got himself a couple of train-robbers and he aims to get them tried and convicted, all loose ends tied. Done the legal way, what happens to us then would be for the judge to decide. What he *seems* to be doin' is going hell for leather down a trail with only the one ending.'

'The two of us dead,' Sean said. 'As fast as possible.'

'In which case, like you said, he's crooked, and must be involved.'

'What about those eye witnesses?'

Luke grinned wryly. 'Did you flag down the Union Pacific?'

'Not unless a rogue engine slipped the tracks and took it up into the Dakotas,' Sean said, with an answering grin.

Then both of them fell silent as, for the second time that day, the passage door slammed open and Cleaver Magg came through brandishing a bunch of keys. Behind him loomed the big deputy, Will Gall. He was carrying a shotgun.

★ ★ ★

The midday sun hit them like a solid wall as soon as they walked out of the jail on to the warped, creaking plankwalk, its heat searing Luke's scalded face and causing the false front of the distant saloon to shimmer as he and Sean gazed in morbid fascination up the long, rutted slope of the dusty street.

Then, as sweat burst from every pore, they were conscious of the silence, and the people: thinly spread, they nevertheless still lined the plankwalks, cowhands in range clothing and businessmen in suits, unshaven loafers holding smeared glasses of beer, ladies in pretty calico with handkerchiefs fluttering at damp brows, drummers in town with their samples and wares, a burly blacksmith in front of his establishment with sleeves rolled up over brawny forearms.

At their appearance the silence broke, and the sudden, swelling murmur from those watchers was like the ominous rumble of a vast, uneasy herd sensing the approach of a lightning storm. Still muted, not yet threatening to become a full-blown roar, yet as Luke fell in behind the shotgunpacking Gall, felt Sean's touch on his shoulder as he stumbled and heard Cleaver Magg slam his office door and stamp on to the plankwalk, he knew that a wrong move would have the effect of stampeding that herd and transforming mild catcalls and insults into a tumultuous oupouring of rage — and the move that triggered the action could come from anybody, anywhere.

'*Here they come!*'

'* . . . thievin' Brennan boys . . . *'

'*Cain't see old Sam Brennan.*'

'*Lookee . . . here comes Judge Flint!*'

'Step it out now,' Magg growled, 'and if you want to live to get tried, don't waste no time.'

They were forced to walk close to the people, to brush against them, striding out up the sloping plankwalk as the watchers pressed back against the buildings or leaped down into the street to trot alongside the fast-moving little procession. Will Gall was ruthlessly using the butt of his shotgun to clear a passage, drawing indignant curses from those slow to move out of the way, but getting them through. The smell of frying beef and onions assailed their nostrils as they passed the open door of a café, and Luke found himself morbidly counting ahead to the meals that remained before that final dawn. A man in wing collar and black tie gazed coldly down on them from the steps of the bank, reminding them of their sins. They strode past the cavern of the smithy where a furnace roared and the blacksmith standing in the open door, either by accident or intent, was idly dangling a chain from one big fist.

Higher up, across the street, the top-buggy that had drawn the onlookers' excited cries had pulled up in front of the saloon, and as the driver set the brake and looped his reins, a dark-suited Reuben Flint stepped down. He cast one swift glance along the street, took in the crowds and the approaching prisoners with their escort, then, with a disdainful jerk of his elegant grey head, he crossed the plankwalk and entered the cool, shaded interior.

'Jury's already inside,' Magg said breathlessly, as Luke turned and spat his distaste into the dust.

'And got their orders,' Luke suggested drily, 'with the promise of drinks on the house if they play ball.'

'They'll listen to the evidence, and make up their own minds.'

'All above board?'

Magg laughed. 'Man, those fellers don't need Flint's guidance. They hear those witnesses tell their story, there's only one possible decision they can reach.'

They were level with the saloon. The crowds had followed, so that instead of thin lines of onlookers on both plankwalks there was now a milling, jostling crowd moving up the centre of the street. Excitement was palpable.

Voices were raised. In the bright sunlight the steel of unholstered weapons glittered.

Will Gall stepped down and started across. Luke and Sean followed. Cleaver Magg went with them, but drifted away to confront the crowd. Luke could hear him talking, but was unable to distinguish the words. Then someone called out, angrily. Magg barked a reply. The unknown voice cut across him, louder, now quivering with fury.

Gall was almost across. Aware of the simmering anger all around them, Luke had let Sean move ahead of him. The half-dozen horses tethered at the rail in front of the saloon were skittish, sensing the tension, eyes rolling and ears flattened as they jerked their heads and pulled back against the taut reins.

Then Magg uttered a sharp oath. Luke turned fast, saw the marshal leaping forward as a man lunged from the crowd, contorted face glistening, eyes fixed on the prisoners. Magg reached him as the gleaming sixgun in his hand came up; swung an arm to slam the edge of his palm down on the extended wrist.

He was too late.

The pistol cracked. Luke felt a mighty blow on the side of his head. Then a thousand stars burst and died to turn day into night and he was weightless and floating with nothing to reach for but blackness.

5

When Luke Brennan regained consciousness, pain was a trapped animal tearing at the inside of his skull, and something like a bear with both arms clamped around his chest was threatening to crack his ribs. He came back to life choking and spluttering, lashed out wildly with both fists and heard glass shatter and a bellow of anger that was drowned by roars of laughter.

He snapped his eyes open and the bottomless pit into which he had sunk became the sunslashed interior of the saloon, the bear's arms the tight loops of a rope tied under his arms and around his upper body and the back of a straight chair to hold him upright alongside Sean. In front of him, the lean cowpoke, who had half drowned him with beer and taken an errant punch for his trouble, was backing off, glass crunching underfoot as he used his bandanna to mop the flow of blood from his broken nose. White-haired Reuben Flint was sitting behind a table some ten feet away across the sawdust-strewn floor, and around the makeshift court the onlookers were packed so tight those unable to find room were perched like buzzards on the rough pine bar.

Luke squeezed his eyes shut, opened them again to meet Reuben Flint's icy gaze. The blacksmith's hammer the judge was using as a gavel rose and fell. The sound as it hit the table was like a gunshot. Laughter was choked off. Gravelly throats were cleared, and there was a noisy shuffling of boots.

'Mr Brennan, you were shot and sustained a minor injury to the side of your head,' Flint said. 'It has been attended to by the doctor, and will cause you little discomfort.'

'Will he be fit to hang?' a voice called, and again laughter exploded and dust motes danced in the sunlight as men furiously hammered tables with their fists.

'Eject that man,' Flint said.

Nobody moved, and over by the bar a cuspidor rang musically as Cleaver Magg spat.

'I guess that's the signal to get proceedings underway,' Flint said, and winked at Magg. Then, perching a pair of gilt spectacles on the end of his beak of a nose, he went on, 'The charges are that Sam Brennan and his two sons, Luke and Sean, did on numerous occasions in the past twelve months rob the Union Pacific railroad of a hell of a lot of money.'

'You gonna hang old Sam, Judge?' the same wag hollered.

'I'll be happy to oblige,' Flint said, 'if you dig him up.'

'Nobody gets hanged,' Luke said, ripping at the knots and flinging the coils of rope into the saw-dust, 'because the charges are trumped up.'

'By whom, Mr Brennan?'

'By the man who made them,' Luke

said, and glared defiantly at Flint.

'That would be Marshal Magg. I spoke with him last night. He's been watching you boys for some time — '

'Been away from town roamin' Montana and the Dakotas, has he?'

'And,' Flint said, ignoring the question, 'he has honest witnesses who are willing to swear — '

'Ain't train robbery a federal crime?'

'Mr Brennan,' Flint said, 'if you don't stop interrupting I will have you gagged.'

'No, sir. In the absence of a lawyer, I'm conducting the defence, and if there was US mail on that train — '

Flint raised an eyebrow. 'Defence? I wasn't aware that there was one. You were seen committing the crimes. How do you defend that?'

'By lyin' his damn head off,' someone shouted, and laughter rippled and swelled.

Flint hammered the table with his makeshift gavel, waited stiffly for silence, then twisted towards the bar and called for a glass of beer. For an instant pandemonium reigned as what seemed like every man present loudly demanded why the bar was closed for them but open for a judge who was getting too big for his boots. Again Flint banged his gavel. The noise subsided to an aggrieved muttering. While his beer was being poured, Flint gestured to Magg and the two men put their heads together and held a whispered conversation. They seemed to come to an agreement, and Magg turned away and pushed through the crowd.

'What chance we got?' Sean said, leaning close to Luke.

'About as much as a candle-flame in a high wind.'

'You're an optimist,' said the sharp-eared Reuben Flint, wiping foam from his mouth and placing the half-empty glass on the table. 'I'd rate your chances somewhat lower than a snake's belly.'

'For Christ's sake,' Sean said in a ragged voice, 'let's get this thing over with.'

Flint raised his eyebrows. 'Now there's a man who's not overly concerned about his future.'

'Or lack of it,' yelled the man who had taken on the role of humorist.

'I'm scared all right,' Sean yelled back, half rising from his chair. He was almost on his feet when two big hands clamped on his shoulders and slammed him back down. Luke turned his head, saw Will Gall, the beefy deputy who had beaten Sean, now standing behind them like something carved out of a hunk of timber.

'My brother's right,' Luke said and, as he reached over with a reassuring grip, he could feel the tremor in Sean's arm. 'Bring on your witnesses, Flint.'

'Marshal Magg,' Flint called.

As the crowd began to part, Luke leaned forward, his lips tight with sudden awareness and the first stirrings of real anger. Cleaver Magg came through from the back of the room. Ahead of him he was pushing a stocky cattleman whose thinning hair was plastered to his glistening scalp as he nervously twirled his sweat-stained Stetson in his thick hands. He was guided to a standing position behind another small table and, when the Stetson had been replaced by a worn Bible, was quickly sworn in by Magg.

'Jake Rawlins,' Luke said, deliberately keeping his voice low. 'Your spread has always been even smaller than our one-horse outfit, Jake. What did they promise you for doing this, a few bucks so's you can buy stock, or as much free beer as you can drink?'

'I had damn near five hundred head of prime beef before the railroad took half my land,' Rawlins blustered.

'Yeah, and you bein' conveniently up against the railroad makes you the ideal witness, puts you in the right place at the right time — '

'I saw what I saw — '

'But how much did they pay you to see something that didn't happen?'

'That's enough!' Flint roared, and for the second time there was the sound of glass shattering as he swung wildly with the hammer and beer and shards of glass flew across the room. This time, there was silence as every man in the room fixed his eyes on Reuben Flint's purple countenance, watched his shaking hand drop the hammer and move towards his hip and waited for the explosion. The silence was broken by the oily sound of a gun cocking. Luke froze as two rings of cold steel pressed against the nape of his neck.

'How do you want it, Mr Brennan?' Flint said, in a voice so tight it squeaked. 'If you object to this witness, would you like the court cleared so that there are none? Would you prefer this session to be conducted *in camera* by Marshal Magg and his deputies? That's one of them holding the shotgun. So is that the way you want it?'

'Magg said witnesses,' Luke said. 'That means more than one. Where are they?'

'We dismissed them as unreliable. Mr

Rawlins is a well-known business-man . . .'

Someone sniggered. Flint paused, swept off his spectacles and stared fixedly in front of him. The snigger became a cough, was as quickly choked off.

'A businessman,' Flint said slowly, 'with a reputation for honesty and integrity.'

'A man,' Luke said, 'just like yourself.'

Reuben Flint's fixed smile was the frozen grimace of a death mask. His chair creaked as he straightened, dragged a hand across a face that was suddenly pale and moist. He reached down, absently flicked a piece of broken glass off the wet table, and looked across at Jake Rawlins.

'Mr Rawlins,' he said, 'why don't you tell us where you were on the thirteenth day of last month. Then tell us how, from that vantage point overlooking Three Mile Cut, you saw Sam Brennan and his two sons stop a Union Pacific train, board it and, in the process of stealing money being transported on that train, gun down in cold blood one of the guards.'

In the awful silence that had settled over the room, the icy blue eyes swivelled. When they fastened on Luke, he saw that they were blank, remote, and he knew that if there had ever been hope of a fair trial, that hope had been quashed by his own rash words.

'When you have listened to what he has to say, Mr Brennan,' Flint continued remorselessly, 'you will be allowed a few brief moments to explain to me why I should not sentence you and your brother to be taken out at dawn, and hanged by the neck until you are both dead.'

6

'He was lying,' Sean Brennan said, 'but, by God, he's the best liar I ever saw!'

The air in the cells was stifling, the sun beating on the roof turning the interior of the jail into a furnace in which the two condemned men had baked for most of the afternoon. They were wrung-out, clothes damp with sweat, heads throbbing. Now, as dusk approached, they could expect some relief, but Luke remembered with bitterness how they had ridden down from the Bighorns with that same exhilarating expectancy of better things ahead, and how cruelly their hopes had been dashed.

'There never were any witnesses,' he told Sean. 'From the minute we walked into the barn and saw Pa, someone's been in an almighty rush to get this thing done with. Over at the saloon,

Flint sent Magg to put words into a man's mouth and cash into his pocket. That man was Jake Rawlins, and he'll stick to his story because along with the cash inducement there would have been a threat.'

And yet, Luke mused, Sean was right: Jake's words had the ring of truth. He had been paid, yes, as his unnecessary bridling at Luke's accusation had made obvious. But maybe the payment had been made not to force him to lie, but to overcome his natural reluctance to betray a neighbouring rancher living through hard times.

If that was the case, then Jake had been pushed forward by Magg to tell Reuben Flint's court what he considered to be a true story: from a stand of trees on his own land and close to the Union Pacific railroad he had witnessed a train robbery; the man leading the three outlaws had been an old-timer name of Sam Brennan; the other two men had been masked, but from their build and manner he was convinced they were Luke and Sean Brennan. The tall, rawboned outlaw — he was willing to swear it was Sean Brennan — had gunned down the guard.

Luke shook his head. 'Pa was always short of a buck, but I can't see him turnin' train robber as soon as we rode over that hill.'

'We know Jake was wrong about us,' Sean said.

'Yeah, so the man he saw wasn't Pa, but looked close enough to him for Jake to jump to the wrong conclusion.'

Sean kicked his feet off the cot and began to pace restlessly. Reuben Flint's casual pronouncement of the death penalty had seemed to settle him. Luke had watched all the obvious signs of fear that had been haunting him since the barn gradually fade, and in the hours since they had been marched back down the street in the blazing afternoon sunshine and flung into the grimy cells he had been resentful, and now puzzled.

'If not Pa,' Sean said, looking through

the barred window at the cool sprinkling of stars, 'then who?'

'Cleaver Magg has to be the one setting this up. Pa's already dead, he wants us hanged, and he wants it done quick. But he wouldn't do the robberies himself, so who was with him in the barn?'

'Lannigan, Stilson. Zak Theaker.'

'Any one of them could've passed for you or me.'

Sean laughed shortly, and turned from the window. 'But not Pa.' He stared at Luke through the strap-steel bars dividing the cells, said softly, 'So who do we know who's Pa's age, Pa's build, and tough as nails?'

'Could be half a dozen old-timers,' Luke said carefully. He knew where this was leading, and didn't like it one bit.

'Come on, Luke,' Sean pressed. 'Jake stood up and named names. If his story's allowed to stand, we get our necks stretched.'

'All right.' Luke came up off his back, sat with his boots planted on the dirt floor. 'Whoever's been doing this is a friend, an enemy, or someone who just don't care either way. But I could sit here scratchin' my head all night, and I'd still come up with just the one name.'

'Fess La Lone.'

Luke nodded. 'Fess La Lone. And I'll tell you something else: when Flint finished his spiel and Magg and Will Gall were marchin' us out of the saloon, that same Fess La Lone was standin' nice and cool at the back of the crowd. He caught my eye — and didn't so much as blink.'

★ ★ ★

At eight that evening, Will Gall came through to light the oil lamp in the passage, leaving them with its weak glow and the warm reek of coal-oil. At midnight he brought them coffee, not bothering to unlock the cells but passing the tin cups of Arbuckle's through the bars. The office door slammed behind him. They drank in silence, listening without interest as the distant tinkling of a piano faded into silence and the occasional horse passed down the street as a cowboy headed for his home spread.

After that they dozed fitfully, as might be expected of a man's last night on earth, one or the other waking every now and then to light the darkness with the flare of a match and the glow of a cigarette. In those waking moments they would listen to the mournful sounds of an owl hooting, a coyote calling somewhere out on the plains; the closer sounds of a man coughing or rattling cups as the deputy on duty did something, anything, to keep weighty eyelids open; and then, when he gave up the struggle, the moist rasping of a man's snoring.

It was Luke who came awake with a start, eyes snapping open, ears straining.

For a few moments there was nothing but the night's velvet stillness and, as the seconds passed, he felt his body begin to relax. Then, from the alley running alongside their cells, he heard the musical jingle of harness, the soft blowing of a horse, quickly stifled.

'Sean!'

His hoarse whisper brought his brother rolling off the cot. In the starlit gloom his eyes gleamed as he looked towards the window.

'I hear it.'

In their separate cells, they waited, scarcely breathing.

Then hands appeared at Luke's window. The end of a rope was passed through, waggled impatiently.

Swiftly Luke crossed the cell, grasped the rope, passed it across the bars and threaded it back through.

Hissing faintly against the iron, the rope was pulled rapidly by the man outside, moving so fast that it was a blur. It stopped. Tightened. Soft commands could be heard. Again a horse blew. The rope's fibres creaked. Timber cracked. Nails groaned.

Then, almost imperceptibly, the whole wall shuddered and began to move.

'When it goes,' Luke said, 'the roof's likely to fall in. Even if it stays put, that deputy and half the town'll come a-runnin', so move faster than you've ever moved in your life.'

'Who's out there?'

Luke's teeth flashed white.

'One of those hands had a finger missing. I recall Fess La Lone once tellin' me how a she-wolf up in the Bighorns — '

A horrendous screeching and rending cut him off. As if sucked out by a powerful summer twister, a section of wall spanning the two cells was ripped away to crash into the alley. Above them the roof sagged. Luke leaped through the yawning gap on to the fallen wall, sensed Sean right behind him, under skies already lightening to the approaching dawn saw the buckskin-clad figure of Fess La Lone fumbling at the hitches securing the rope to a saddle-horn.

'Out front!' the old-timer yelled, 'horses at the rail,' at the same time slipping the rope free, vaulting into the saddle and spinning the horse towards the street.

Behind them the passage door banged as the deputy, dragged rudely from sleep, came charging through. The man saw what had happened, yelped in surprise and went for his gun. Luke spun away, raced for the corner and ran into the street. La Lone was already away, his mount kicking up dust as he headed out of town at a gallop. At the rail, two horses were loose-hitched. And, Luke saw, there was a gunbelt looped over each saddle-horn.

A light flickered in the general store across the street as they freed the reins and flung themselves into the saddle. A shot cracked from the alley. Luke ducked. A bullet whined over his head. Then they had wheeled away from the jail, spinning the excited horses on a

68

dime. Hooves thundering, they hammered up the slope through Fess La Lone's settling dust. A man in his underwear appeared on the plankwalk outside the saloon. A shotgun blasted, and buckshot hissed through the air.

But the wicked sound of its passing was behind them and, swiftly, to the fading echoes of angry cries and the occasional futile crack of a sixgun, so was the town of Linch.

They were free, and running.

7

They headed north, the three men coming together as Fess La Lone reined back, then again spurring their horses so that the fierce drumming of hooves on hard-packed earth was to each man his own pulse thundering in his ears.

For Luke and Sean the excitement of the flight after the unexpected release from captivity was infectious, but the heady exultation that sent fierce rebel yells ringing through the night from throats still dry with nervous tension was driven close to hysteria by the thought of the chase.

Cleaver Magg would raise a posse.

He would do it in fury, and in haste.

And with what seemed like a reckless disregard for their own safety, they were going exactly where Magg would expect them to go.

'Why this way?' Sean called, swinging

in close to Luke as euphoria ebbed and common sense prevailed.

'Because to find out what's going on,' Luke yelled, over the wind roaring in his ears, 'we need a place to start.'

'Pa's dead, he can't tell tales.'

'No, but we arrived so sudden I doubt his killers had time to cover their tracks.'

Sean nodded, wheeled away with his hand clamped to his Stetson as Luke pushed ahead to where Fess La Lone was streaking down the trail on his ragged claybank mare.

A quick sidelong glance from brilliant blue eyes in a nest of fine lines was his greeting. From then on the two men rode together in silence, with Sean an outrider staying clear of their dust and flinging frequent nervous glances over his shoulder. After two hours at that steady clip they caught the glint of Crazy Woman Creek in the increasing dawn light, topped a rise thick with jack-pine and swung north-east for the run in to the one-loop spread old Sam

Brennan had named Dorado.

They arrived like the vanguard of a stampeding herd, hammering across the yard as if the posse was already snapping at their heels. Luke's inclination was to tie up in front of the house, but La Lone gestured with a wide sweep of his arm and they rode on down the slope, hooves deadened by the straw underfoot as they drew rein in the cool shadows inside the barn where the removal of Sam Brennan's mutilated body had done nothing to eliminate the raw scent of death.

Luke stepped down, trailed the reins and let his horse wander. La Lone had beaten him to it, his gelding with the big Sharps .50 poking out of the saddle boot watching calmly with its head turned as the hunter moved away to swing the big double doors shut. Sean was out of the saddle and soothing his nervous mount, his mind only half on the job and his face pale in the gloom as his eyes probed the shadows.

'I heard that apology for a judge talk

a heap of nonsense,' La Lone said. 'Where the hell is your pa, Luke?'

Straw rustled as the feisty hunter came across to confront him, standing like a bareknuckle prizefighter, right leg back, left shoulder forward and chin tucked in as his gaze switched between the two Brennan brothers.

'We found him not too far from where you're standing,' Luke said. 'Magg let us bury him out back before he took us in.'

'He was alive yesterday, for sure,' La Lone said. 'I rode down from the Bighorns for the first time in a year — '

'Day before,' Sean said, and his hand strayed to his throat. 'Hard to believe but another day's dawned, Fess, and round about now — '

'Quit that, goddamn it, you're wasting time feeling sorry for yourself and we've got precious little!' La Lone fumed. 'I saw Sam from the ridge, he gave me a wave. There was no mistake, so what the hell happened?'

Luke shook his head, stepped towards

the buckboard, poked his toe into the stiff, blood-stained straw.

'Somebody cut him to pieces and left him here to die, Fess.'

'Since when did a mysterious somebody mean you and Sean?'

'Since circumstances made it look that way. A couple of hours before we got home, I used Sean's Bowie to put a trapped deer out of its misery. They saw the dried blood.'

'They? You mean Magg and his cronies? What were they doing here?'

'When we rode in there was no sign of them. We spent some time looking for Pa in the house then came over here — and they jumped us.'

'Hah!' La Lone's voice registered disgust. 'That sounds like Cleaver Magg's customary way of operatin'.'

'Yeah, but whether what he did is right or wrong depends on your point of view,' Luke said. 'If him and his men rode out here all legal to arrest Sam and found him dead they would have been more than a mite jumpy, and that knife did look suspicious.'

'You sound as if you're arguin' for him, 'stead of against.'

Luke shook his head. 'The law ain't perfect, and people like Cleaver Magg and Reuben Flint have no place in the system. But throw them out of the picture and you've still got trains being robbed, Jake Rawlins testifying to what he saw — and now the two fellers suspected of those crimes have bust out of jail.'

'Which means Magg'll be justified if he orders his posse to shoot you on sight.' La Lone nodded, his blue eyes thoughtful. 'But what about your pa? If we take a couple of long paces back from where we're at right now, we're still lookin' at an unexplained death.'

Sean laughed softly. 'Mulling things over in that cell, your name came up twice, Fess. Skinning knives would have done a clean job on Pa, and Jake's pretty damn certain it was an old-timer he saw robbin' that train.'

'And he got the name wrong?' Fess

La Lone grinned sardonically. 'Well, maybe if I'd thought of it and wasn't so doggone lazy . . . ' He sucked his teeth, let his eyes go distant as he cocked his head to listen for a few moments in the settling silence, then said, 'And what about Jake's testimony? Seems to me the only part of that trial that didn't stink to high heaven was his story.'

'Pa's no robber,' Luke said.

'But for some damn reason someone wanted him dead.'

'I can't figure it.'

'The way he was worked over,' Sean said, 'it could've been Indians,' and his bruised face tightened at the memory.

La Lone shook his head. 'You know as well as I do they're peaceable right now.'

'Well, whoever killed him rode in from somewhere, then rode out again,' Luke said. 'Like I already pointed out, I doubt he had time to cover his tracks.'

'So we look around,' said La Lone.

'And do it fast,' Luke said. 'Magg will have been pushed to raise a posse, but with full daylight he won't wait around.'

'Something else you should worry about,' La Lone said. 'You were right about this being a federal case. Deputy US Marshal Tom Carson is the lawman leanin' on Magg. He rode west aways, day before you hit town. But he'll be back, and Magg'd like nothing better than you two strung up and out of the way before that happens.'

★ ★ ★

When Luke and Sean Brennan came down from the Bighorns to splash through Crazy Woman Creek and ride into Dorado it had been like entering a ghost town in which the only sign of life was the restless stirring of tumbleweed tangled against the barn's sagging walls.

Within fifteen minutes of walking out into the clear after-dawn light, Fess La Lone was able to tell them that Cleaver Magg and three men had ridden in on the wrong side of the corral and tethered their mounts in thick scrub behind the barn. From there they had skirted the yard on foot to come at the house from different directions. When they returned to the barn, the four men had become five.

That fifth man was Sam Brennan, he told them, and old Sam had walked to the barn. As far as he could tell, those five men had been alone on Dorado — but, he reminded them, his reading of sign had been hasty because he was doing it with one eye to the ground and the other looking over his shoulder.

The old hunter's fixation with the posse was making Luke jumpy, and so far they had discovered almost nothing that they didn't already know. Time was running out, but they couldn't leave.

'We're no wiser,' he said, clattering up the steps and into the house.

''Cept we're even closer to pinning Pa's murder on Cleaver Magg,' Sean said.

He'd left Luke and Fess La Lone to the tracking and was in the deep shadows at the far end of the big living room, sitting on a swivel chair and poking around on the scarred roll-top desk old Sam had used for everything from paperwork to mending bridles.

'What's that you've got?' said La Lone.

'Well . . . ' Sean's face was troubled. He glanced at Luke and handed him a crumpled piece of paper. 'I half wish I hadn't found it. It don't make good reading.'

Figures. A place name. Luke smoothed the paper and tilted it towards the window, felt La Lone looking over his shoulder, heard the soft, explosive 'Christ!' as the old-timer's sharp blue eyes took in the damning words.

'A timetable,' Luke said, feeling a sickness rise in his throat. 'Someone wrote down when the Union Pacific westbound was due at Three Mile Cut.'

'But not Pa.'

'No, this writing ain't his.'

'But it puts the robbers right here in this room,' La Lone said.

Luke's snort was dismissive. 'Tell me

what chance an old man alone's got if armed men walk into his house.'

'Armed men?' Sean's came up off the chair, anger in his eyes. 'Don't pussyfoot, Luke. That still leaves us with Magg, Stilson, Lannigan, Zak Theaker.'

'The only one at the trial,' Luke said thoughtfully, 'was Magg.'

'Only one needed,' La Lone said. 'Stilson and Lannigan are town bums. Zak Theaker's something else. Sharp gunslinger. Too friendly with Reuben Flint. If they're in this with Magg, Theaker would know to lie low until after the trial.'

Sean had moved restlessly to the open door and was now out on the gallery staring towards the ridge. The birds that had noisily welcomed the sun as its warm light flooded the yard and pushed back the shadows were silent. A board creaked as Sean's weight shifted, and a muscle in Luke's arm twitched.

'These armed men,' he said, 'what would they do if they rode from here to

Three Mile Cut and robbed the westbound?'

'Ride right back again,' La Lone said positively, 'and stash those money bags.'

'Here?'

La Lone pursed his lips, dragged a tobacco sack and paper from his shirt pocket and began rolling a cigarette. Luke went to the desk, idly riffled through the litter of papers, picked up a telegraph slip. Behind him, a match scraped and the flame's light washed over the paper. He folded it and put it in his pocket. Then he went outside, touched Sean's shoulder, and from the end of the gallery looked back across the yard towards the barn and the rough country beyond.

'Yes, here,' La Lone said, the smoke from his cigarette swirling as he joined Luke. 'Are you thinking what I'm thinking?'

'They hitched their mounts behind the barn because they'd stashed the money way back in the scrub.' Luke said slowly. 'Then, for some reason, they came across to the house for Pa, took him to the barn — and someone with the mind of an Injun began using a knife.'

'I'm beginnin' to see it,' Sean said. 'The money wasn't where it should've been.'

'No,' Luke said. 'Pa had moved it, and they tried to make him talk.'

'What I figured,' Fess La Lone said, 'but for the life of me I can't see why.'

'When we rode in, we thought Pa wasn't there to greet us because he didn't get my wire.' Luke reached into his pocket, brought out the telegraph slip, passed it to Sean. 'He did. I don't know how or even if he was involved in this mess, but because he couldn't bear for us to see what was going on, he paid with his life.'

8

They were jumped as they searched for the bulky canvas sacks that had to be buried in the wild tangle of scrub behind the barn, the strengthening sun beating down on them and a hail of bullets zipping through the already sweltering heat as Magg's posse came yipping and howling into the thickets with sixguns blazing.

But the formation of that posse was surely a terrible indictment of Cleaver Magg's guilt for, clearly desperate to move under a shroud of secrecy, in his efforts to catch the fugitives he had recruited not a single new man.

Using the same tactics that had ensnared Sam Brennan, Magg sent Stilson and Lannigan around to east and west to come crashing in from the flanks. He'd also brought along Deputy Will Gall, maybe figuring that the big man's fists had so imprinted themselves on Sean Brennan's memory that it would give the deputy an edge.

Maybe it did. Gall took the direct line, charging in from the barn with thorny chaparral ripping at his pants and his shotgun held high, blued barrels flashing in the sun. Already ducking and weaving under the hot lead spraying at him from both sides, Sean took one look at the big deputy on the glistening black horse, and scuttled for cover.

But he wasn't the first to go.

His own pistol out and blasting, Luke turned to where Fess La Lone had been sniffing out tracks with his sharp eyes skinned for fresh-turned soil, and couldn't see him. Like the Teton Sioux through whose sacred lands he ranged and hunted, the rawhide-tough mountain man had simply melted into the landscape.

Cursing, salt sweat stinging his eyes and thorns tearing his sleeves as he turned again to face the attackers, Luke loosed another shot at Will Gall — and suddenly felt a glimmer of hope.

Before leaving the yard he'd insisted they move their mounts from the barn to an outcrop of tree-crowned, rocky high ground half a mile behind Dorado. Their search for Sam Brennan's cache of stolen money had been conducted on foot, moving steadily away from the jagged bluff and back towards the barn. On foot, they were able to work their way through the scrub, at times ducking low to scramble through dust and debris where twisted branches, hidden from the sun, had withered and died.

Cleaver Magg's posse, on the other hand, was rapidly beginning to understand the plight of a burr caught in a woollen blanket. Without tough leather chaps their legs were being ripped by razor-sharp thorns, or held so fast the man was near pulled from the saddle. They'd pointed their horses into thick brush at a run, seen their mounts make twenty yards only to finish up thrashing madly to stay in one place.

Bitten off more than they can chew, Luke thought. But he also knew that before too many more seconds ticked away he had to turn their stupidity to his advantage.

Stilson and Lannigan were already out of the saddle, their horses snorting as they struggled to back and turn. Will Gall roared his anger, let go both barrels of his shotgun and went tumbling off his horse with a crash like falling timber.

As Luke turned away and began to thread his way back through the scrub, he caught a fleeting glimpse of Cleaver Magg and Zak Theaker. They'd stayed back near the barn, the tall gunslinger standing high in his stirrups with a Winchester up and ready, Magg turning his big sorrel first one way then the other as he squinted into the flying dust.

Then Luke was down low, forcing a way through the brush below branches thick with live thorns, unable to see ahead but always with the hot sun on the back of his neck to tell him he was heading for the bluff.

Deep in the scrub there was a thick, eerie silence, the sounds of the posse coming to him like distant voices in a waking dream. The healing wound on the side of his head throbbed, his damp shirt was clammy on his back. He pushed on, feeling a trickle of blood where a thorn had torn his cheek. The dust kicked up by his own slow progress was thick in his nostrils, his sixgun too hot in his hand.

Then, out of nowhere, a figure reared up almost on top of him, white face glistening, eyes wide with shock. Luke's breath caught in his throat. He swung his pistol, had it cocked and his forefinger squeezing the trigger when he recognized Sean's lean frame. With a strangled grunt he tilted the .44, felt the muzzle blast hot on his face as the bullet winged skywards. And from close, too close, triumphant cries rang out.

'Jesus Christ!' Luke said.

'God, I thought I was done, then I thought you were Fess, then . . . hell, I don't know what I thought. Where *is* Fess?'

'Lit out, like we'd best do if we want to stay alive.'

Swinging away, sleeving his face and spitting dust, Sean gasped, 'I guess they're too stupid to realize they could just set out there and wait for us to die of thirst.'

'Take too long,' Luke said. 'Easier for Magg and Theaker to ride around this brush and wait for us to pop out under the bluff like rabbits out of a hole.'

A pistol began banging, over to their right. Bullets snicked through the branches. Another man opened fire to their left. Caught in a deadly crossfire, they tucked their heads into their shoulders and stumbled on in a painful half-crouch, half-crawl. A bullet plucked at Luke's shirt. He swore, grinned in sweaty reassurance as Sean glanced back.

The firing stopped. Luke reached forward, grabbed Sean's shirt, pulled him to a halt. Hearts thundering, fighting to quieten the rasp of their breathing, they dropped to one knee, facing away from each other as they listened to a man talking at the outer limit of hearing range.

'That's Magg,' Luke said at last, his hand still fast on Sean's shirt.

'I heard, but not what he was saying.'

'He was telling his cronies in the brush he's about to do what I expected him to do. But before him and Theaker set off to circle round and cut us off, he's doing what we're doing: listening.' He looked up through the branches at the fierce sun, twisted his head and said, 'Can you see the bluff?'

'It's close.'

'Yeah, that's what Magg's afraid of.'

'If we move now, he'll hear us. Do we go for it?'

'Damn right we do.'

With the hand holding Sean's shirt, he gave his brother a shove. As he did so a rifle cracked, and Sean grunted, deep in his throat. Luke felt the shock through his hand as Sean's whole body jerked. Then the bunched cloth tightened and began to slip through his fist as Sean started down. As he did so the two pistols opened up, and Luke turned aside spitting as dirt kicked into his face.

'Oh God, not you, Sean!' Luke groaned.

In the heavy silence, Magg and the mounted gunslinger had been watching as well as listening. Their sudden movement had been spotted and answered in deadly fashion by Zak Theaker and his Winchester.

Luke lunged forward, slipped an arm around Sean's back and under his arm and felt the hot sticky wetness of blood. Still down in a crouch, knees cracking with strain, he held him up, urged him on; heard the boy whimper through clenched teeth, clenched his own jaws in the beginnings of despair.

Then, from high on the unseen

rimrock, a big gun thudded.

Fess! Luke thought, and his heart leaped.

Deep in the scrub, a cry came, as swiftly died with a terrible gurgle.

Four, five seconds — and again that powerful thud.

And Magg's voice, high and tight with anger: 'All of you, pull back!'

Again the big Sharps thudded. This time, the whirr of the heavy slug parting the air could be heard close by and, to the sound of brush crackling, the nearest of their unseen opponents began a hasty retreat.

The accurate fire from the hunter's buffalo gun was driving the posse back. With his mouth close to Sean's ear, Luke whispered words of encouragement, tried to blank his mind to the blood now soaking his sleeve. He urged him to walk forward, then swore softly and braced himself as the boy tried to respond and almost dragged Luke down as his legs refused to support his weight.

Grunting, Luke changed his grip, ducked down, took Sean's full weight across his shoulders and eased himself upright. As thorns tore at his brother's clothing he poked his head out into bright sunlight and saw that the gamble had paid off. In front of them, the chaparral thinned rapidly. They were almost in the lee of the high bluff.

He lurched forward. In six steps he had carried Sean clear of the tangled scrub and stood with his boots on springy grass. Behind him he could hear angry voices, the snorting of a horse. Defiantly, a sixgun cracked. The slug hissed over Luke's head. Then, like a grotesque echo of that shot, the big Sharps thudded. Someone cried out, and a sudden rattle of hooves moving away told Luke that, for the moment, they were out of danger.

But there was no way up the almost vertical cliff face on the Dorado side. To get to the horses Luke would have to take Sean the long way round, and to keep the posse at bay while Luke carried Sean clear, Fess La Lone was forced to remain on the bluff.

'Fess!'

'I hear you!'

'Keep me covered!'

The laugh from the heights was without any humour.

'You can count on it, boy!'

Luke took a deep breath. 'This ain't going to be easy,' he said, and wondered with wry amusement if he was warning Sean, or talking to himself.

Then he set off.

In fifty yards he was soaked with sweat. Along with the sweat he could feel the warmer stickiness of blood. Each step he took drew a whimper of sound from Sean. Each time a boot hit the ground he felt the weight across his shoulders shift, and tightened his grip.

For those first fifty yards across an easy slope he moved at a fast walk. Then he turned towards the high ground, the incline steepened, and he moved into the trees. Suddenly there was debris underfoot. He slipped on a dead branch, felt Sean begin to slide, half fell against a stout trunk and wedged the wounded man between his back and the tall timber.

Sean groaned as, grunting, panting, Luke eased him back into position.

'You OK?'

'Mmm.'

'Soon be there.'

A lie.

Luke lurched away from the tree, fought for balance, gained it by turning into the slope and taking a couple of stumbling steps upwards. Then he began the long, uphill struggle, taking his time now but from necessity not choice. Each step was like lifting feet shod with boots of lead; each breath drawn was agony. His heart thundered in his chest, threatening to burst, and Sean's weight was gradually forcing his head down so that he had to strain to see where he was going through eyes awash with salty sweat.

How was he keeping going? He had no idea. What he did know was that after a certain time he reached the limit of his strength, struggled through it and still kept moving. The rasping, throaty whimpers were now his own, not Sean's. The blood he tasted was his own blood, for in the mighty struggle he had almost bitten through his lower lip.

Suddenly, it was over. A horse whinnied close by, the trees thinned and, as the ground levelled, he staggered out into bright sunlight. Then Fess La Lone was alongside him, together they lowered Sean to the ground, and Luke was able to straighten his creaking back. He stood, eyes closed and hands on hips, sucking in great gulps of air. Gradually, the pain faded. After a while, the trembling in his limbs stilled.

Luke Brennan sleeved away sweat and blood.

He opened his eyes.

Sean was on his back in light shade at the fringe of the trees. La Lone was down alongside him, on his knees, the big Sharps abandoned. The hunter had ripped open Sean's shirt; the exposed chest was like a glistening red carapace.

'Throw me your bandanna,' La Lone said, and ripped his own from around his neck.

Luke's throat tightened.

'He bad?'

'We're stuck here, Luke. I got Stilson but, while you were carrying Sean up the hill, Theaker and Lannigan worked their way round to the east so they're behind us. Magg and Will Gall are still over by the barn. I can make sure they stay there — '

'You didn't answer my question.'

'But that's only until darkness. Come nightfall the four of them'll be together at the bottom of the hill and then it's a matter of time before they storm through them trees.'

'Goddammit, Fess!'

The hunter looked up, his steel-blue eyes flashing.

'All right. Theaker's Winchester slug went in under the right arm, maybe punctured a lung. Maybe. I ain't sure.

Now, you do like I said and pass me your bandanna — no, make that your shirt — then I'll patch him up as best I can and, for what it's worth, your brother'll live.'

He wadded his bandanna into a ball, caught the shirt as Luke stripped it off and tossed it to him, and began to tear it into strips.

'But I don't think you were listening, Luke,' he went on, busy with his ministrations. ' 'For what it's worth' means it ain't worth a plugged nickel. I can patch your brother up good as new, but the whole exercise is pointless because not a one of us is going to get off this bluff alive.'

Part Two

Flesh and Blood

Part Two

Flesh and Blood

9

By late afternoon, La Lone's canteen was empty. Almost all of the lukewarm water had gone to Sean, moistening his dry lips or cooling his fevered brow. The only horse with anything in the saddle-bags other than dry pigging strings, tobacco dust and a rusty horshoe was the tough little claybank, which belonged to the hunter. The others had been stolen from the livery barn at Linch and saddled with rigs hastily snatched from rails before being led to the alley alongside the jail.

The sun had taken its time passing overhead. In the scorching heat of the afternoon, Luke had suggested sharing spells with the Sharps, but La Lone would have none of it. He had spent most of the late morning lying on the slight upslope that ran to the rimrock, and remained there through the after-noon, watching the barn with an eagle eye and, from time to time, looking along the gleaming barrel to let loose a single thudding shot that gave Magg and Theaker the clear message they'd best stay put.

Sean had recovered consciousness when the sun was directly overhead, his eyes blinking open to stare into the dazzling light filtering through the tangle of branches. He had been in pain but rational; had told Luke that his breathing seemed OK, and had drunk greedily every time the canteen was held to his lips. The bleeding from the wound in the side of his chest had been staunched, but his face went from pale to flushed as time passed, and his eyes had a distant, glassy sheen that kept Luke chewing his lip in worried indecision.

Most of the time, Luke had prowled. Hell, he couldn't think of a better word for it! Some of that restless moving around had taken him into shade beneath the timber on the northern down slope. Once, he'd gone a mite too far downhill and drawn a shot from either Lannigan or Gall that had thunked into a tree close enough to flick a chunk of bark into his hair, and he knew they were as alert as the wily old hunter.

Then, around the time when in normal circumstances they would have been considering lighting a fire to prepare a sizzling evening meal, Magg and Theaker began to have fun.

La Lone had just got back from his own restless wanderings that had taken him to a section of the woods more to the east. He had been away some time, had returned with a look on his face that Luke couldn't fathom — but then bullets began to fly, and the moment was lost.

'Pa's long rifles,' Luke said as shots rang out in slow succession, and the accurate fire from 800 yards chipped fragments from the rimrock and showered them with dust.

'Broke into his rack, got their hands on that Hunsicker Long Rifle,' La Lone said, nodding. 'Well, I expected some such around this time. Letting us know time's running out.'

They were lying on their sides at the top of the incline leading to the edge of the bluff as gunfire rattled and slugs whined overhead. Sean had jerked out of a doze at the sudden noise, twisted his head to look towards the rimrock and been given a reassuring wave of the hand by Luke.

He was safely out of earshot.

'Seems to me,' Luke said, 'the kid's getting weaker.'

La Lone's eyes were expressionless. 'So time's running out in every way possible.'

'If he hadn't taken that slug — '

'We could've gone before now,' La Lone finished for him. 'Three of us against them two down there would've been highly favourable odds.'

'Could still be done,' Luke said, 'if you can hold Magg and Theaker at dusk. You keep them occupied while I get Sean on his horse. It's half a mile from the barn to the bluff, some way more than that around the scrub to the bottom of that slope behind us. It'll take time after you quit shooting for Magg to realize we've made a move, more time to get here. By the time he does, we'll have taken those two bums down there and be well on our way.'

'Hey, Luke!'

Sean's voice was weak. When Luke turned, he was up on one elbow, watching them.

'Hell, I thought you couldn't hear.'

Another crackle of gunfire from the distant barn drew the wounded man's eyes to the trees as bullets hummed overhead.

'Enough to know what's goin' on.'

'You up to it?'

'I reckon can stay in the saddle, hold a pistol.'

La Lone shook his head. He wriggled to the rimrock, poked the Sharps over and fired a single shot. When he rolled on to his back and used his feet as a V-sight to look towards Sean, his face was sceptical.

'Biting off more than you can chew at this stage is risky, son.'

'How about lyin' here and waitin' for Magg to come get me?'

La Lone grinned. 'That's another option I wouldn't recommend.'

'But it's one or the other,' Luke said.

'No,' Sean said, and met his brother's eyes. 'There's a third.'

'Don't even think about it.'

'You two could make it. I can handle that old Sharps. While I hold them, you . . . work your way down through the woods, drive the horses one way and slip . . . past them on foot.'

Fess La Lone glared. 'You think I sprung you from jail so's you could give yourself up? Any case, all you'd do is delay the inevitable. Magg'd come up here and finish you, then take off after us. You intend takin' on the whole posse?'

Luke nodded, again looked at Sean.

'Besides which,' he said, 'I'd say you'd have trouble holding that big rifle level.'

In the deepening shadows under the trees, Sean's smile was wan.

'Yeah,' he said, and suddenly there was no pretence as the weakness he had been fighting to hide drove him down so that he was once more flat on his back, his shallow breathing barely moving his bandaged torso. 'I guess that sounds like the best option after all, me settin' there, you doin' all the work . . .'

His voice trailed away. From the barn, a single rifle cracked, and for the first time a sixgun answered from the bottom of the slope.

'Making a point,' Luke said softly. 'Letting us know they're there, waiting . . . and that brings me to a fourth option.'

'Let me guess,' Fess La Lone said, and his eyes gleamed. 'You both give yourselves up?'

Luke nodded slowly. 'When did you say this US marshal's due back?'

'I didn't.'

'But he outranks Magg.'

'Christ, Luke, Magg ain't here, so rank don't count — '

'If I put it to Magg, tell him we'll throw down our guns if he hands us over to Deputy US Marshal Tom Carson — '

'No!' La Lone's teeth were bared in a snarl of frustration. 'You're clutching at straws, boy. Magg wants you dead before Carson gets back. You walk down that slope, he'll cut you down. If Carson asks questions he'll say you were resisting arrest.'

'Now it's you not listening, Fess.' Luke tried to keep the weariness, the resignation, out of his voice, but knew he had failed. 'It's not a fourth option, it's the *only* option. All this talk of Sean holding them off while we make a break, of three of us taking our chances up against those gunslingers — it's all nonsense. There'll be four men down there, one man up here's got a slug in his chest — and, damn it, we both know he's not strong enough to sit in a saddle.'

And suddenly, sick of the useless discussion that was getting them nowhere, he drew his sixgun and fired three measured shots into the air.

'You got us out of jail,' he said, 'and I thank you for that. But things have changed, one slim chance for Sean is better than none, and for his sake, I'm taking it.'

★ ★ ★

Night fell like twin curtains, blanketing the east but letting through the soft crimson glow of the sun that was fast dying in the west. On the bluff, men and trees became indistinct shadows in the eerie light. Below and to the north, Crazy Woman Creek was marked by a thin white mist hanging low; the scrub extending half a mile to the barn was lost in blackness, the barn itself an irregular tall shape rimmed with red.

The reverberations of Luke's three

shots had scarcely died away when, like an echo, three answering cracks were heard from the direction of the barn. Fess La Lone had wriggled to the rimrock with his field-glasses, told Luke that Magg and Theaker were out and mounted, but taking no risks.

'They got glasses?' Luke had asked.

'I reckon.'

'Tie something white on the end of that Sharps, hold it up.'

La Lone did so, with reluctance. It brought a single shot as acknowledgment.

'They're on their way,' La Lone had said moments later — then lapsed into a silence that had yet to be broken.

'You ready?'

Sean was up on his horse. In the face of La Lone's stubborn silence, Luke had managed to get the wounded man into the saddle without help. Despite Luke's conviction that Sean could not sit in the saddle, he was staying there by sitting slumped forward with both hands folded on the horn. He had guts, and Luke figured that a slow ride downhill could be managed.

'If we're goin',' Sean said, 'better do it now.'

'Before you fall off?'

The answering grin was a flash of white teeth.

'All right,' Luke said, 'let's go.'

He swung into the saddle, waited for Sean to move his mount at a walk across the dampening grass then cut in front of him and led the way into the trees. Still the hunter said nothing. He had come down from the rimrock, ripped the white rag from the Sharps and thrust the long rifle into its saddle boot, and the last Luke saw of him before he was lost in the darkness and the trees closed in behind them was the glint of those steely-blue eyes as La Lone turned to watch their departure.

They let the horses pick their way down, instinct guiding them back to the trail where they had left droppings earlier that day. Once or twice Sean grunted with pain as his mount stumbled. Each time Luke glanced back, jaw tightening, expecting to see the dark shape tumbling to the ground.

It didn't happen. The slope levelled, and in a crackling of dead branches they emerged from the trees. As they did so there was an explosion of movement all around. Riders closed in from either side, forcing Luke and Sean together so that stirrups touched.

A hand reached out, grasped a cheek strap, pulled Luke's mount to a halt.

'Where's La Lone?'

This was Cleaver Magg, easing his mount forward in front of them with Zak Theaker close behind.

'You don't want him,' Luke said.

'Aiding in a jail break, killing a deputy. Damn near pullin' down my jail.' Magg laughed. 'He'll get so used to a prison cell he won't want to leave.'

'He's . . . long gone,' Sean said. There was a tremor in his voice. He turned stiffly to spit.

'But you two . . . ' Magg's voice was puzzled. He touched his mount with his heels and moved close to Sean, leaned over to look in his face. He grunted. 'Is this why? Your brother's shot, you figure you reach town I'll let the doc look at him?'

'That, and a fair trial,' Luke said.

'Man!' Zak Theaker breathed softly. 'You ain't goin' anywhere near town.'

'Two men broke jail,' Magg said. 'I formed me a posse, pursued them as far as Dorado, caught them in the scrub back of the spread. In the ensuing exchange of shots — '

'Dead,' Luke said, appalled. 'You're talking cold-blooded murder.'

'No sir. We apprehended escaped train robbers, at considerable risk to members of the posse. Judge Reuben Flint'll like that.'

'Hell,' Theaker said, 'we'll be in them newspapers back East.'

At Luke's side, Deputy Will Gall said, 'Rider coming. Kinda sneaky.'

Theaker cursed.

'Fess La Lone,' Magg guessed, and glanced at Luke. 'Is this what you planned?'

'No, dammit,' Luke said tightly, 'you've looked hard enough at my brother — '

'Take their pistols!'

Gall and Lannigan moved in, jostling. Luke turned on Gall, furious, and there was an oily click as Theaker worked the lever on his Winchester. Rough hands plucked six-shooters from holsters, tossed them into the scrub. The gunmen moved away.

'Leave then in the open, then — '

A branch snapped, and Magg's head jerked around. The rider was coming in fast along the lee of the bluff. Theaker swung his horse towards the sound. Lannigan and Will Gall melted away, bridles jingling.

'I told you,' Sean said, 'Fess La Lone's gone.'

'Then who . . . ?'

And then the rider was upon them. He came in at a steady canter, a black shape looming large in the darkness, the badge pinned to his vest glittering.

'Tom Carson,' Cleaver Magg said,

and the frustration in his voice was like music in Luke Brennan's ears.

'I ain't heard so much fireworks since Bull Run,' said Deputy US Marshal Tom Carson. 'What the hell's going on here?'

10

The ride across the prairie from Dorado to Linch took them more than four hours, Sean appearing to grow weaker with each tough mile, Tom Carson doing his best to keep the pace of the long ride even and personally ordering posse members to hand over their water canteens so that the wounded man had plenty to drink.

Luke rode as close to his brother's horse as he could, now and then steadying Sean in the saddle, relentlessly keeping him talking in the belief that allowing him to lapse into unconsciousness would be fatal. But, as the eyes drooped and the answers took longer to come, he knew his efforts were cruel and from then on kept his peace. After that Sean dozed fitfully and, to Luke, his breathing seemed maybe not stronger, but certainly easier.

The deputy US marshal rode at the head of the group with Cleaver Magg, Zak Theaker was a few yards back, Gall and Lannigan together behind the prisoners. The town marshal was sure to be spinning a yarn over and above the stark details of the jail break, but what it might be Luke neither knew nor cared. Tom Carson was a federal lawman with the backing of the Senate. Cleaver Magg was unlikely to buck that kind of authority.

'Luke?'

It was close to midnight, the breeze cool at their backs, the moon a thin, silvery crescent hanging high above the weak yellow oil lamps lighting Linch's main street. Sean's eyes were unnaturally shiny, his voice thin and infinitely weary as they cut across the wagon ruts and rode down the dusty slope into town.

'Yeah, I'm here.'

'I just realized, they can't put us back in that jail.'

'No, I reckon not, but Magg'll have a

secure place lined up. With Carson around, he's forced to.'

'I was right, wasn't I? Magg's a crook.'

'Him *and* Flint. But I can't figure out if they act that way out of habit, or if they're tied in with those train robberies.'

'Ain't no doubt, it's the robberies,' Sean said, and Luke sensed that the bullet wound that was draining his brother's strength had brought a clarity of thought that was beyond most men. Death was lurking in the shadows. In those circumstances . . .

'Not Flint.' Sean was shaking his head. 'But Magg, yeah, and he ain't finished with us.'

'Let it lie,' Luke said. He gently cuffed his brother's shoulder, drew a courageous grin and was forced to look away, swallowing the lump in his throat.

There was a sudden rattle of hooves as Will Gall broke away from posse and prisoners and cut across the street towards the smithy. By the time the rest of them arrived and tied up at the rail his hammering had woken the blacksmith. Towering over the big deputy, he had come out of his room pulling on his pants and stood in his undershirt, knuckling sleep from red-rimmed eyes.

As he listened to Gall, then shook his head irritably and lumbered away to drag open the smithy doors, Magg came over to Luke.

'Get him down, and inside.'

'They fixin' to keep us *here*?' Sean said, as Luke helped him out of the saddle, standing close to take his dead weight and ease him down to a shaky standing position as Magg watched impassively.

Tight up against Sean, Luke whispered against his ear, 'How you feelin'?'

'Nowhere near as bad as I look.'

Then Tom Carson was with them, tough, angular, a .44 butt forward on his left hip, and Luke stepped away. The federal man's words were clipped, precise.

'Your partner's still out there. According to Marshal Magg, he'll try to bust you loose again. If he does, he'll find you shackled together so tight he'll need to carry you out in one piece.'

'What's Magg been telling you?'

'Very little I didn't already know.'

Luke stared the federal man in the eye. 'Did he tell you that when you rode up out there he was fixing to shoot us down in cold blood?'

'That's a lie,' Magg said, 'but no more than I'd expect from a man fighting for his life.'

Luke was still holding Carson's gaze. The federal man's face was expressionless, but the grey eyes were shrewd and he seemed to be taking his time weighing up the situation.

'Whether or not,' he said now, and drew a hand down his bushy moustache. 'I'll be talking to Judge Flint — '

'They were tried and convicted,' Magg said. 'There's nothing to talk about except when and where they hang.'

To Luke, there seemed to be two separate conversations going on at the same time, one between him and Carson, one between Carson and Magg. In some strange way, neither seemed to be connected; it was as if the federal man was standing in the middle with an open mind while accused and accuser made their case. In answer to Luke's question, Carson had said 'very little I didn't already know'. That suggested he knew a damn sight more than he was letting on, and Luke found himself wondering what this lawman had discovered while he was out of town.

Carson and Magg moved away, still talking. Will Gall hollered from the smithy, and the bronc buster came over with a grin and used his .44 to shepherd Luke and Sean inside.

The blacksmith was at the bellows, a massive figure shiny with sweat that glistened red in the lurid light as he worked to get the glowing coals in the forge up to white heat. Still grinning,

Lannigan moved them back beyond the anvil, and for ten minutes they watched as the blacksmith got the temperature he required and fashioned shackles, the black anvil ringing to the mighty blows of his hammer, the intense heat rising from his forge to fill the small workshop, and Sean with his mouth hanging open, visibly wilting.

But how much of that was a sham, Luke wondered, as Sean glanced his way and an eyelid fluttered in a wink.

Was he feigning weakness? If he was, could they play on that?

'Lannigan!' Luke yelled over the din. 'Go tell Magg my brother needs a doctor.'

The bronc buster spat, and turned away.

And when those ten minutes had passed and another ten dragged after them and they walked out into the chill night air that hit their overheated bodies like a blast of winter, Luke was connected to Sean by a short length of chain linking the fetters that had been fixed about each man's wrist.

'I'll talk to Flint tonight,' Carson was saying to Magg. They came away from the hitch rail, the federal man's shrewd eyes taking in the shackles, the deputy and bronc-buster flanking the prisoners, the blacksmith closing the doors on the glowing forge and heading back to bed. 'For now, you get these two locked away . . . back of the livery barn, right? . . . I'll mosey along to the telegraph office, then out to Flint's place, be back as quick as I can to check everything's secure.' He hesitated. 'I want a deputy or someone with them at all times. Can you fix that?'

Magg nodded. 'If you're sending a wire that'll take time, try your patience. The operator's deaf, always drinks like a man just come crawlin' out of the desert. If he stayed late in the saloon . . . '

He let the words hang, flashed a look at Zak Theaker. Luke intercepted the glance, saw the cunning in the town marshal's eyes that was there, then gone, as he swiftly averted his gaze.

'He'll hear me,' Carson said, and smiled thinly.

'What about the doc?' Luke said, again drawing attention to Sean's weakness. 'You taken a close look at my brother? He's got a rough dressing over a bad bullet wound. He needs medical attention, fast.'

Carson glanced at him, looked critically at Sean, and a thin smile touched his lips as he nodded. 'I'll pick him up on the way back. Your brother's still on his feet, and there's not much the sawbones can do with you two out in the street. So the easier you make this for Marshal Magg, the quicker your brother gets attention.'

He nodded to Magg, untied his horse and stepped up into the saddle, the rattle of hoofbeats echoing flatly from the false fronts as he swung away and set off for the telegraph office.

The livery barn was at the eastern end of town. They had passed it on the way in, a wide building with double doors and horse trough standing at the top of the grade that dipped steeply from the town's outskirts before easing to a gentle downhill slope. Luke wanted to ride, pointed out to Magg that Sean was in no shape to go climbing mountains. But Magg was in a hurry, and the way they were shackled together he could see no easy way of getting them into the saddle — and he was damned if he was going to lift them there!

They made it fifty yards up the silent street, struggling through alternating pools of lamplight and shadow, Sean lurching one way then the other over the uneven ruts, the iron shackle dragging painfully at Luke's wrist. Then, when Sean stopped and sagged to his knees under the rail outside the saloon, Magg impatiently ordered Lannigan and Luke to get his arms across their shoulders and walk the exhausted man bodily the rest of the way.

And still it wouldn't work!

'For Christ's sake,' Luke cried. 'His

left arm's shackled to my right. How in God's name can I get that up over my shoulder without snappin' my own arm off!'

Fretting and fuming, glancing over his shoulder to look back down the street, Magg was finally pacified by Lannigan. The tough bronc-buster stepped in, crouched, and came up with Sean across his shoulders.

'No!' Sean protested. 'Goddammit, I can walk — '

'Leave it, Sean, take the easy way,' Luke cut in. Something stank to high heaven. Magg was as jumpy as a drop of water on a hot skillet, and Luke knew he had been wrong: the marshal was prepared to buck any kind of authority.

He watched Lannigan set off, and knew that even that short break would help Sean: if they hit trouble and were forced to fight their way out the boy would need all his remaining strength. Yet after another fifty yards, even Lannigan was finding the combination of Sean's weight and the wagon ruts too much for him. Grunting with effort he lurched sideways and, dragging Luke with him at the end of the chain, stepped up on to the plankwalk, and with that more even surface underfoot they made it the rest of the way up to the barn.

Theaker was already there, having ridden his own horse and led Sean and Luke's. All three horses were loose hitched at the rail, and he was dragging open the big doors. Magg went inside, banged on the door to the hostler's living quarters, yelled, 'Comin' through, Vinny!' and took the irate hostler's stream of abuse without blinking. He walked off down the dark runway. Theaker, casting a black look behind him, ordered Lannigan to watch the prisoners and went after Magg. Straw rustled in the stillness, and the soft sounds of dozing horses coming awake marked their progress past the rows of stalls.

Inside the barn, Lannigan had roughly dumped Sean, left him swaying but on his feet, and closed one half of the double doors. The bronc buster was standing against the wall, panting, but his eyes never left them and his pistol glinted in his big fist. When Luke glanced beyond him, the street was empty: Will Gall was not with them, and had probably crossed the street to the jail.

They were guarded by just the one man.

Without making any sudden movement, Luke began to edge away from the gunman.

'Magg's in too much of a hurry,' he said softly to Sean.

The boy had been leaning forward, legs spread and hands on knees, breathing through his open mouth. Now the chain linking them clinked as he went with Luke.

'Carson'll be gone for some time,' he said huskily. 'Right now, we're as good as dead.'

'If Magg's going to do it, it's got to be before we're locked up.'

'Make it look like an escape?'

At the far end of the barn a door opened.

'There's outbuildings back there, make a good cell. The alley back of the barn runs the whole length of the street.'

'Too narrow,' Sean said. 'They'd pick us off easy — and our horses are out front.'

'Maybe that's their idea. They down us there Carson'll take one look, figure we broke, foolishly ran along that alley, got plugged. So . . .'

Lannigan had come away from the wall, and was moving towards them.

'You two,' he said. 'Quit that talking.'

Luke glanced over, said quickly to Sean, 'So it's got to be here.'

'I said quit that!' Lannigan moved in, stepped close enough to ram his pistol into Luke's back.

At the same moment, Magg called from the end of the barn.

'Lannigan! Bring them on down.'

'Right, move yourselves,' Lannigan said.

With a sideways glance at Sean, Luke took a couple of fast steps that carried him forward and away from Lannigan but into the deeper shadows cast by the closed door. Then, as the chain between the shackles snapped tight, he deliberately stumbled and went down on one knee. Sean was pulled towards him. His right leg bumped into Luke.

Still behind them, again moving closer, Lannigan growled impatiently.

As if to help himself up, Luke grabbed for Sean's belt with his left hand. Covered by the curve of his body, his right came around and dipped into Sean's boot. His fingers curled around the hilt of the big Bowie. He took a swift breath, held it, then exploded into action.

With the knife in his hand he came up and spun outwards on toe and heel. He whirled with his right arm extended and curved and the gleaming blade held horizontal. Lannigan was caught flat-footed. Luke came around fast, straightened his arm, continued with the wide, flat sweep. The razor-sharp blade slashed bone-deep across the bronc-buster's throat. He staggered back with bulging eyes. Blood gushed, became a transparent red curtain swept wide by the Bowie as it followed through. Then the strength went from the gunman's legs and the .44 fell from lifeless fingers as he crumpled, breath bubbling.

'Let's go!'

The surprise attack had taken mere seconds, in deep shadow. Deceived by the faint rectangle of light that was the open half of the big doors, Luke guessed that Magg would have seen nothing. As he stooped to slip the bloody knife into Sean's boot, the marshal's impatient call made that clear.

'For Christ's sake, Lannigan, get a move on!'

As the cry echoed up the runway they ran for the doors, Sean now striding faster than Luke, the shackle pulling tight against Luke's already raw wrist as his brother loped ahead of him and they headed for the horses. Outside, they ducked under the rail, turned, and Sean took the horse on his left, grabbed the horn with his left hand and swung into the saddle. Luke reached forward to slip the hitched reins. Then, awkwardly, shackled left arm pulled sideways and up by the chain, he found a stirrup and stepped up into the saddle.

A startled yell from the barn told them that their dash into the street had been seen.

'You sure you're up to this?'

Sean's answer was to lift the reins high, rake with his spurs and swing away from the rail so hard his horse barged into Luke's mount and sent it snorting into the street. Dust billowed under flashing, dancing hooves. Locked together they made the middle of the street, pointed the horses towards the town limits. As the excited horses began to stretch out, they drifted apart. Shackled arms snapped straight. The strain on shoulder sockets threatened to pull them from the saddle. Quickly they came together, settled to ride stirrup-to-stirrup.

Angry voices rang out from the barn. Downslope, from the jail, a man yelled. A rifle cracked, and a bullet whispered overhead. Then they were over the crest and running as buildings thinned and the cool breeze from the open prairie was in their faces like the cool fresh taste of freedom.

11

'We should have rode double!' Sean yelled, his face twisted in a grimace as he looked with hatred at the short iron chain linking their outstretched arms.

'On one horse, they'd catch us within a mile.'

'If they come after us.'

Luke's laugh was sardonic, torn ragged by the wind.

'This time, they'll come. If they don't, that federal man will — and Magg won't take that risk.'

The bright sliver of moon floated in a sea of stars. The lights of Linch's main street were behind them, the trail ahead cutting like an arrow through the town's outskirts. They bore down on a familiar house with white picket fence and veranda, and again lamplight glowed warmly in an upstairs window and a dark figure could be seen. But

134

this time he was not alone. A horse was hitched to the fence and, at the thunder of their rapid approach, two men rushed to the ornate rail and, as faces caught the pale light of the moon, on one man's chest a badge glinted.

'Carson,' Luke said. 'Keep your head down!'

They hurtled past in a rattle of stones and a cloud of dust, the angry bellows of Judge Reuben Flint like a swarm of bees buzzing irritatingly about their ears. For a hundred yards they raced on, then continued for another breathless 200 before Luke dared to glance back. When he did, he saw light flooding from the open front door and a tall man caught in it like a moth, running for his horse. But beyond that lone figure, other horsemen could be seen, coming like the wind. Luke counted three, even at that distance saw the glint of Zak Theaker's Winchester and guessed that the other riders were Gall and Magg. The marshal had brought with him the inner circle of his band of thieves, and that inexorable pursuit caused Luke Brennan to shiver with apprehension.

They pushed on at breakneck speed across gently undulating terrain made treacherous by ancient wagon ruts that in the wan light were deceptively shallow, always aware that if a horse put a foot wrong and one man went down he would drag the other with him and all would be lost. But the pace could not slacken. When, after a hair raising mile and a half, Luke again twisted to look back, he saw that the pursuing riders were holding station but were still just three in number.

'Carson stayed behind,' he said. 'Goddamn it, that man trusts Cleaver Magg — and that's our undoing.'

'Not yet it ain't,' Sean said; and something in his tone drew Luke's eyes to the youngster's face. There was defiance in the words, but the timbre of the voice had changed. Zak Theaker's bullet had gone in under Sean's right arm, and since their flight from Linch the constant pulling of their linked arms had reopened the wound, soaking his shirt with fresh blood. Now, the voice Luke listened to with a terrible foreboding was the voice of Sean as an infinitely weary young boy: the weakness he had so stoutly denied had drained his face of colour as it overwhelmed him, and in the draining transition from life to death it was giving him back the illusion of his childhood.

'No,' Luke said gruffly, 'damn right it ain't.'

Around them as they pushed on, night sounds were increasingly deceptive. The thunder of their horses' hooves was unremitting, but to Luke it seemed that the faint, far-ranging sounds of the pursuit came from one direction, then another, as if bands of phantom horsemen were loose on the prairie and closing in from all sides.

At the same time, Sean's horse was becoming increasingly uneasy as its rider sank into semiconsciousness. It began to toss its head and veer from its course, and Luke's attention was constantly distracted from the menacing, moonlit shapes that were the three following riders as he struggled to hold his own seat, pull Sean's horse back in line and keep the boy in the saddle.

It was a ride out of a man's worst nightmares, the likely outcome unimaginably horrific.

Half an hour later they hit the Powder and took their horses through the ford in a scintillating shower of spray, the sudden dousing in ice-cold water reviving Sean and jerking him upright. But his strength had gone, and the far bank almost unseated him. Luke hung on, jaw tight, jostling his horse close to lean across and hold on to his brother's shirt as the horses lunged up the slope.

Cottonwoods and aspen were thick along the bank and beyond as the trees tenaciously followed the course of many deep winter run-offs. And they were closing in on that welcome cover —

were within a few yards of the trees — when Sean grunted, arched his back and began to topple sideways.

An instant later Luke heard the flat thud of the distant rifle.

Instinctively, he threw himself sideways and flung his right arm awkwardly across to slam Sean forward across the horn and along the horse's neck. Somehow he held him there and kept his own seat, using knees and spurs to drive his horse hard against Sean's and force the reluctant animals into a wide swing that carried them off the trail and into the trees.

They went in with a snapping of branches, the horses snorting their disquiet as they were forced away from the cool water. Luke urged them onwards, his weight on his left stirrup, his arm flat across Sean's back. The horses were tight up against each other and, with the raw strength of his arms and legs, he kept them like that for forty yards, used his right spur to drive them another desperate twenty. Then, inevitably, luck ran out and the frightened horses parted and went either side of a solid tree. Luke's shoulder slammed into the trunk. His arm, already blood-soaked, was ripped away from Sean and, as the horses crashed on through the woods and the chain linking their fettered wrists snapped in a tight loop against the tree, they were both plucked backwards out of the saddle.

Sean hit hard. Luke landed cat-like, but was dragged down into the carpet of dead leaves as Sean flopped like a heavy grain sack. A quick wriggle took him to his brother's warm body. He lay there, his right hand feeling for the throb of a pulse in the throat, his head twisted as he sniffed the cold night air and listened above the rasp of his breathing for the approach of riders.

Nothing. The fading crackle of twigs as their two horses walked away through the cottonwoods. The liquid murmur of the river.

No movement beneath his questing fingers.

Luke took his hand from Sean's throat. Chain links clinked as he rolled him on to his back. He put his ear to the boy's face, listened; wet the back of his hand and put it to Sean's nostrils and prayed for the coolness of living breath.

Nothing stirred.

'Oh, goddamn you,' Luke said softly, and came up on his knees and rocked back on to his heels.

But who was he cursing?

Zak Theaker.

Twice the man had slammed the butt of his Winchester into his shoulder, squeezed the trigger and shot Sean. This time he'd killed him. But Theaker was directed by Cleaver Magg. The wickedness didn't begin when the trigger was squeezed, it began when Magg and his band set out to rob the Union Pacific and became obscene with the killing of Sam Brennan.

That was the beginning, that was

where it had led, and it must go on; for the end to be complete there had to be three killings. And there would be three killings, Luke thought, unless he took the fight to Magg; unless he went after the man, and discovered the truth.

A reliable witness had sworn that Sam Brennan was a train robber, aided by his sons. A town constable given a marshal's badge and turned crooked had arrested the suspects. A shady lawyer elevated to the position of judge had — for reasons that could only be underhand — convicted and passed sentence.

None of that had anything to do with the truth.

Those bastards, Luke swore, didn't know the meaning of the word.

All right, by God, then they'd learn!

But first, like the deer they had encountered as they rode down through the Bighorns in the ruddy light of evening, it would take a knife to cut him free.

He dragged a hand across his face

and felt the wetness of tears he had been unaware of shedding; inched forward through the leaves on damp knees, hesitated — and again reached down to his brother's boot.

Then froze as somewhere out in the moonlight beyond the trees, metal jingled. A man's voice whispered, was answered. Water splashed, and a pebble rattled.

Like the deer they had found trapped and frantic, Luke's head turned left, right, eyes staring, ears straining. He heard the horses clatter up out of the river trailing water, heard the muffled thud and slither of hooves on soft earth as they lunged up the bank. Then he waited, teeth bared, hand instinctively slapping his holster — and finding it empty! Waited for the sudden outburst, the excited shouts, the rush of approaching men, that final hail of bullets.

In those tense moments his thoughts raced. He realized that when they forded Powder River, he and Sean had turned sharp left from their direction of travel; to enter the woods had swung left again. That first turn and the river crossing had put the thick stands of cottonwoods between them and their pursuers. They had entered the woods unseen, and the trail ahead twisted sinuously so that for some miles, even in daylight, a man passing along it would be out of sight to another riding 200 yards back.

And this was night, and there was no reason for Magg to suspect that he and Sean had not pressed on towards Dorado.

The Bowie knife came out of Sean's boot with the silken sound of metal against leather. On it, on the hilt and on the broad, heavy blade, there was the stickiness of Lannigan's blood. Luke felt that tackiness, wrapped his fingers around it, forced them to close. And with the knife again in his hand he remembered the wide, sweeping slash, the gush of warm blood that sprayed the straw and the walls of the livery barn, the ghastly bubbling of a dying man's breath.

Luke swallowed. He raised his left wrist until the chain tightened, moved his arm to one side and felt his stomach churn as Sean's dead right arm followed, swaying. He lowered the arm into the leaf-mould; reached down with his left hand to grasp the warm forearm close to the iron shackle; turned his face to the sky and squeezed his eyes shut as his lips moved in silent prayer.

Like an episode from a ghostly dream he could hear the muted rattle of hooves as mounted men passed by. There was bile at the back of his stretched throat, a tenseness within him that was causing his body to hum like tight wire and his mind to become detached. He took a deep, shuddering breath, opened his eyes to the tangled canopy of branches, the high sprinkling of distant stars.

Then he bent over the arm and with his sight blurred by unshed tears he put the heavy blade to the soft flesh below the base of the thumb and cut off his brother's hand.

Blood welled thickly. The shackle slid from the stump. With trembling fingers Luke picked up the severed hand, tucked it inside Sean's shirt. Then he rocked back and stood up and, with a sudden surge of violent emotion, he drew back his arm and sent the big Bowie flickering end over end through the trees.

It took him half an hour ranging back and forth to collect enough rocks to cover Sean's body, some moss-covered, some still wet from the river. At the end of that time he was drenched with sweat but his mind was working normally and, as the last stone rattled on to the crude grave and silence settled over the woods, he heard the sounds he had been expecting.

Cleaver Magg was returning.

And now Luke was alone, on foot, and unarmed.

12

As the drum of hoofbeats swelled into a rapidly approaching tattoo, Luke turned reluctantly away from his brother's makeshift grave. Swiftly, he picked his way through the trees to the edge of the woods some way closer to the river than where he and Sean had entered. The chain still attached to his wrist clinked against his knee as he dropped into a crouch and looked out across the grassed slope that fell away to the broad, silver ribbon of the Powder, and was now lit eerily as the sickle moon slid behind high, thin cloud.

In that wan light, shadowy figures riding out of the distance across a strangely shadowless landscape came hammering back along the snaking trail that led north-east to Dorado, Magg out front closely followed by Zak

Theaker with big Will Gall trailing some way behind.

Luke had expected them to head for the river to seek the tracks they had ignored in their blind certainty that the fugitives were making for home. Instead, Magg made straight for the woods and rode along the edge, his figuring being, Luke guessed, that there was only one place they could have gone, and two mounted men would have left some scars on the brush in their wild dash to get under cover.

As the dust of their thunderous approach drifted and settled they searched methodically, Zak Theaker working away from the river, Magg riding along the fringe of trees all the way down to the muddy bank. But it was a sweating Will Gall coming up late who made the discovery, and he did it by dropping heavily from his horse in his urgent need to respond to a call of nature and damn near falling flat on his face over the branches snapped off by Luke and Sean.

'Magg, Zak!' he yelled. 'Over here, we got 'em!'

His pistol came up, its cold glint winking as he took a pace deeper into the woods and swung one way, then the other, as he peered into the dark thickets. Then Magg and Theaker arrived, earth flying in clods as they brought their horses to a skidding halt and tumbled from the saddle.

'They left Lannigan's pistol,' Theaker said, breathless, clinging to the reins as his big black horse pulled back.

'And we dumped theirs in the scrub back of Dorado — so they're unarmed.'

Luke heard the grudging satisfaction in Magg's voice, but detected none of Will Gall's certainty. Cleaver Magg was smart enough to know that finding where the fugitives had entered the woods merely revealed how they had slipped away from the posse. Time had passed, and he and his cronies had wasted too much of it following an empty trail and retracing their steps. Magg knew it was unlikely that their quarry would have waited around for their return, and his instant relief at picking up the trail was quickly replaced by ruthless efficiency.

'All this'll get us,' he said, 'is some idea which way they went.'

Scrub crackled under his boots as he stepped into the timber. Gall grunted a protest as he was roughly pushed aside. Zak Theaker reached back to the saddle boot for his Winchester, left his horse ground-hitched and followed Magg.

Luke heard the snick of Magg's pistol as it was drawn and cocked, but the three men had stepped from open ground lit by luminous night skies into the darkness of the woods, and were also hidden from his sight by the intervening trees and scrub. All he could do was listen to their noisy progress, knew they would follow the trail he and Sean had left: broken branches; a carpet of dead leaves churned up by the horses; the final white scar where the chain's links had looped around the trunk of a cotton-wood and thrown them to the ground.

But when they found Sean's grave — and no sign of horses — they'd know that Theaker's Winchester had found a target, but done only half the job.

So then what?

Twigs snapped like gunshots. All three men were cursing as they blundered deeper into the cottonwoods. They were moving away from Luke, and Luke's immediate reaction was to make the distance between them greater by moving in the opposite direction. The only sensible way he could go was out of the woods. He came up out of his crouch. Branches clawed at his pants as he stepped out on to the grass. The night breeze cooled his face, and he sniffed the earthy wet tang of the river.

As he stood up and stretched the stiffness out of his cramped frame he recalled that, when he and Sean had been thrown to the ground, their horses had crashed blindly on through the woods. They were likely to have kept going until they hit open ground. But would Magg find the grave, then follow those tracks, assuming that Luke was riding one of the horses? Or would he return to where the posse's horses had been left and ride around the woods in the hope of picking up the trail?

Luke's guess was that he'd play safe, send one man ahead while the other two came back for the three horses. But which one? And the grave was, what, sixty yards away? Which gave him almost no time.

But even while his thoughts were racing, he was moving. The posse had left their horses ground-hitched. Luke had his eyes on the rangy black ridden by Zak Theaker.

He took Sean's bloodstained shackle in his hand to silence the clanking and broke into a jog up the slope, slipped on the damp grass, heard raised voices and knew that the men in the woods had stumbled on the grave. Now Magg would look ahead, see the sign left by the fleeing horses, and make up his mind.

Time was running out.

Panting, Luke reached Theaker's black horse, put his hand out to snatch at the trailing reins as its head shot up and it began to turn — and missed. At the same time, he heard the sound of the posse returning, and knew that coming back out of the woods they'd be much faster.

His sudden approach had spooked the other horses. Magg's and Gall's were already thirty yards away, trotting downslope towards the river. But the big black was made of sterner stuff. It had stopped, and turned its head to stare inquisitively at Luke. He clicked his tongue softly, took several careful steps, said, 'Easy, boy,' — and lunged for the reins.

This time he got them. The big horse backed, then swung on him, white teeth nipping playfully at a shoulder. Then Luke had found a stirrup and stepped up into the saddle. With the reins held high he wheeled the big horse and kicked it into a canter, then a fast gallop. He pointed it up the slope, started towards the winding trail and heard the crackle of scrub and Cleaver Magg's sudden bellow of anger. A pistol cracked, then again, and Luke bent low, gritted his teeth, and hoped that Magg had sent Theaker on through the woods.

His hopes were dashed as a rifle barked. Two rapid shots followed. Bullets hissed overhead, the second one close enough to clip his Stetson. Then came a third, and Luke gasped in agony as fire raked his ribs. For an instant his vision blurred, and sickness welled as the world spun dizzily. He shook his head, fell forward, grasped the black's flying main and clung on.

Then he had reached the first snaking turn in the trail that dipped into a hollow and around a stand of trees. He rounded them at breakneck pace, heard a final rifle shot that sent a bullet winging wide of its mark, and let his breath go as the black's smooth, raking stride carried him out of danger.

* * *

The blood from the wound across his ribs had trickled down into his pants. It was soaking his thigh, and he was sitting in a sticky pool. His head sang with weakness. The black's smooth gait was shaking him to the bone.

On top of the constant pounding and the weakness that was threatening to drag him to a standstill was the worry that taking one of the horses would not have slowed the pursuit. Magg and Theaker would have caught the mounts that had strayed towards the river, and ridden away from Will Gall.

The black was fast, but for some time Luke had been forced to hold him back. He was finding it difficult to stay in the saddle. The wound needed binding to stop the loss of blood — but halting before he reached Dorado was too risky.

'Easy to say, but hard to avoid.'

He caught himself mumbling the words and realized he had snapped himself out of a doze. A quick look back over his shoulder almost had him out of the saddle. He clung on, looked blearily about him, saw the grey light of dawn as an almost imperceptible lightening to the east.

Then he was off the broad trail, rocking in the saddle as the big black took over and with flaring nostrils headed through the long grass towards a pool that glinted at the bottom of a deep hollow where the high lip and rocks exposed by centuries of erosion afforded some cover.

'Goddamn sneaky animal!' Luke mumbled with enough affection to move him to tears. He waited until the horse had high-stepped across the soggy ground to the moss-covered pool and had dipped its muzzle into the cool water, then slid from the saddle with a groan. His head spun. His mouth was parched. He clung to the horn, glanced with distaste at the scummy water then remembered that this was Theaker's horse. His shaking fingers made hard work of the buckles, but when he got the saddle-bag open he found an almost full canteen.

The water, ice-cold from the breeze washing over the saddle-bag during the fast ride from the Powder, poured strength into his body and cleared his mind enough for him to realize that his sluggishness had been eating away the minutes. He listened, heard . . . but what did he hear? The soft soughing of the breeze in the long grass? The gentle whisper of his own pulse? The big black's contented breathing, or —

Panic brought cold sweat to his brow, sent him clambering desperately on to one of the big rocks, narrowed his eyes as he feverishly scanned his back-trail.

And discovered, with a feeling of bleak dismay, that he had finally run out of time.

13

Cleaver Magg and Zak Theaker were less than half a mile away, and Luke cursed his lack of foresight in not taking time to move the big black horse out of sight. Thirst slaked, it had wandered away from the pool and his pursuers had seen it outlined against the lightening skies. Even as he watched, they veered off the trail and into the long grass and spurred their horses in an arrow-straight line towards the hollow.

As he leaped down heavily from the rock and felt his legs buckle beneath him, a feeling of numb resignation washed over Luke Brennan. It lasted but a moment. He staggered, regained his balance — and found himself suddenly consumed by anger, and the burning desire to survive. In that fraction of a second it occurred to him that such is the nature of the human spirit that the conscious realization that death is but the whisper of a bullet away serves to jolt the unconscious instinct for survival into action. It sent Luke running for the black, drove him into the saddle with his arm clamped to his wounded side and, as enraged shouts rang out behind him, he kicked the refreshed horse into a surging gallop and raced out of the hollow.

He knew he would be caught. To leave the dip he was forced to cut left across Magg's line of approach, and that lost him precious seconds. By the time the big black breasted the lip and Luke swung him towards Dorado, Zak Theaker had passed Magg and was closing fast. Luke's fleeting glance backwards told him that, this time, Theaker had forsaken his Winchester. This was close-range work: his pistol was in his hand and, as Luke turned away and settled to his task of coaxing from the gallant horse speed, and yet more speed, the first shot rang out.

The bullet hissed by, its closeness flattening Luke along the black's neck and starting a fresh flow of warm blood as the wound ripped open. A second shot cracked and Luke used his knee to push the horse into a violent swerve that almost unseated him. He drove it across the wide trail, pulled it back as pain knifed through his ribs and his head swam. But even that manoeuvre had lost him precious yards. Now he could hear Theaker's horse, snorting with effort as it pounded down on him. A snatched glance showed him Theaker, off to one side but preparing to draw level, the man's black eyes glittering, his teeth flashing in a savage grin of triumph. His pistol was raised, but he was taking his time, working in close before firing that single, fateful shot that Luke would not feel, nor hear.

Then he was gone.

As if digging into reserves of strength, the gunman's horse surged alongside the black — but now the saddle was empty. Then, stunned by its unexpectedness, Luke heard from far up ahead the solid thud of the big Sharps Buffalo. Even as the unmistakable sound sent his spirits soaring, he felt the wind of a bullet that buzzed wickedly past his ear and heard Magg's yell of fear that was punctuated by the sound of that second shot.

And when Luke risked another glance behind him, he saw Magg falling back, desperately cutting at an angle towards a stand of trees as a third shot thudded.

The pursuit was over. The way to Dorado was clear.

★ ★ ★

It seemed to Luke that he was forever destined to arrive home with the rising or the setting of the sun. Again he rode in with the dawn, weakened by loss of blood but seeing in the cluster of buildings a sanctuary where he could rest and restore his strength for the fight that still lay ahead. For, despite

Fess La Lone downing Zak Theaker and putting Cleaver Magg to flight, that situation was but a temporary respite.

Magg was the killer of old Sam Brennan, and must pay for his crime. More, he must be forced to admit his complicity in the Union Pacific robberies, and remove from Luke the threat of the hangman's noose by taking it on himself. Only then could it be said that justice had prevailed — though even that important victory would be a hollow one, Luke acknowledged, with his father and brother dead.

Those thoughts were in his mind as he bore down on Dorado, and at once sensed that something was wrong.

Wearily he drew rein, sitting stiff in the saddle. Why wrong? How wrong? Fess La Lone's rifle had fallen silent once Magg had withdrawn to cover, and Luke had pushed on, making only one brief but necessary stop to apply a rough dressing to his wound. Had Magg also pointed his horse towards Dorado and, in those chill hours before dawn, overtaken Luke — perhaps when he was off the trail, gritting his teeth against the pain of tearing his stiffened shirt away from the raw wound? Was he now holed up, waiting, Theaker's Winchester at the ready, perhaps choosing the barn for the ambush so that Luke would die where his father had fallen?

But those were fleeting thoughts that Luke listened to absently while letting his eyes range over the familiar buildings. And even as he listened they were swiftly dismissed: Dorado was silent and undisturbed; the premonition of something being amiss had come not from in front, but from behind.

Suddenly he was conscious of the drum of hoofbeats that had impinged on his subconscious, slyly alerted him without pinpointing the danger. He twisted in the saddle, saw Magg closing, bearing down on him, spun and kicked the black into a walk that swiftly became a gallop towards the yard — but was too late. Magg was on him. He was shouting, his voice thick with rage as he came alongside and drove his horse up against the black. Legs slamming together, horses twisting to snap at each other with bared teeth, they clattered across the yard towards the house. Magg reached for him, not with his pistol but with his clawed bare hands, snatching at the chain dangling from Luke's wrist — and, as if punched in his middle, he bent from the waist and was swept from the saddle.

Again the eerie whistle of a bullet, the sickening thwack as it hit human flesh followed almost instantly by the distant thud. This time, the sound of the shot came from the bluff. Luke heard the solid thump as Magg hit the dirt, saw the marshal's horse veer and go trotting towards the barn — and was bewildered.

What the hell was Fess playing at? Why was he up on the bluff?

Then he felt the black stiffen under him. It was already crumpling at the knees when the second thud of the

Sharps .50 came floating from the bluff. Luke hit the dirt rolling, his teeth clamped against the pain, and for the first time since taking the horse, it gave him cause for regret: Fess had recognized the big black, and thought its rider was Zak Theaker — and now Luke was rolling into dangerous open space away from the downed horse, aware of the hawk-eyed hunter up on the bluff with his finger preparing to squeeze the trigger as he looked along the sights.

'No, Fess!' Luke roared, knowing his voice wouldn't carry the distance, couldn't carry the distance. He clambered to his feet through a red mist of pain, lurched into a crouching run that took him staggering and swerving towards the house, reached the gallery steps and fell on them as a bullet kicked up dust behind him. The boards were hard up against his bony hip. He rolled on to his back, gasped with relief, then closed his eyes and thanked the Lord as he looked to the side and saw that the edge of the house was now between him and the bluff and knew that the bullet Fess had drilled into the dust was the closest he could get to the man he believed to be the last of the posse.

Zak Theaker was dead. Cleaver Magg was dead. Stilson. Lannigan. The only man left out of the bunch was Will Gall. It was over.

And a voice from the house said, 'You about ready to do some talking?'

14

Tom Carson had the stove going, the room rich with tobacco and wood smoke, the black coffeepot's lid rattling away on top of the head of steam and two tin cups ready. He was pouring the strong black coffee as Luke walked in, carried the cup to him as he sank into a chair and dragged a sleeve across his damp face.

I rode in and didn't even notice the smoke, Luke thought. What the hell's wrong with me?

'Loss of blood does that to a man,' Tom Carson said, as if reading his mind. 'Skews up his thinking.' The grey eyes were examining Luke, taking in the bloodstained shirt and pants, the healing wound on the side of his head, but where Luke had expected the severity usually meted out to the criminal he saw understanding, and something close to compassion.

'One thing I know for sure is the fellers who robbed those trains are all dead, except Gall,' Luke said, gingerly sipping coffee. 'Cleaver Magg, Zak Theaker, Stilson, Lannigan. Damn near every one of them involved in those robberies. Fess did me a favour, gunning them down when he did, but if Gall's lit out . . . '

'It might be difficult proving your innocence?'

'Impossible.'

'Maybe Jake Rawlins'll talk, admit to being bribed to testify to something he didn't see?'

'I think he was, but he'd have to be bribed again to admit it.'

Carson shrugged enigmatically, fired up a cigarette, blew a plume of smoke.

'What happened to your brother?'

'Theaker got him. Him and that damned Winchester.'

'How?'

Luke took a deep breath, looked reluctantly at painful memories. 'We crossed the Powder in moonlight, headed for the timber to lie low. Theaker's shot took him in the back, he was dead when he got dragged off his horse.'

'How come they didn't flush you out of the trees, pick you up there and then?'

'They didn't see us go in. We cut left when we came out of the river, left again into the trees.'

'If they couldn't see you, how did Theaker shoot your brother?'

A silence settled over the room. Luke sipped the scalding coffee. His mind was sluggish. He tried to think back to the ride out of Linch, recalled hearing sounds from all around and how, in his weariness, he had pictured phantom horsemen. But phantoms couldn't hold a rifle, squeeze off a shot. Zak Theaker must have worked his way around to the flank so he could see them. But if he could see them, he'd know where they'd gone . . .

'I don't know,' he said.

Carson nodded slowly. 'So,' he said, 'your brother's dead,' — he looked at the chain dangling from Luke's wrist, the dried blood on the loose shackle, and nodded with tight lips — 'you got away and headed for Dorado — right?'

Luke smiled bitterly. 'A mite more complicated, but that about sums it up.'

'Then what happened?'

'Fess La Lone again. Theaker rode up on me, Fess blew him out of the saddle, then tried for Magg.'

'You sure about that?'

'I *know* it,' Luke said. 'That slug whistled so close I felt the draught.'

'All right,' Carson said, but his shrewd grey eyes had narrowed. 'After that you made it here, Magg damn near caught you, and this time La Lone downed him. But why did he shoot that horse out from under you?'

'I was riding the black,' Luke said. 'Theaker's horse. In this light, from that distance, it was a natural mistake.'

'Not if he'd already *downed* Theaker,' Carson said. 'Downed Theaker — from a distance, remember, which says something about his eyes — then sent a slug so close you damn near caught it in your teeth.' He examined the glowing end of his cigarette, said softly, 'There were two men out there favouring long guns: one of them's dead, the other's up on that bluff and the bullets are still flying.'

'Goddamn!' Luke said through clenched teeth. 'What the hell are you sayin', Carson?'

'I asked you if you were ready to talk. Now I'm asking you if you're prepared to think.'

'Fess La Lone got me and Sean out of jail. Up on that bluff, he was dead set against us givin' ourselves up — '

'You stopped to think why he got you out of jail in the first place?'

'He's an old friend, goddammit!'

'Where's he been for the past twelve months?'

'The man lives by hunting. He was away for a year, same as us, he told me — '

'No!'

Luke blinked. The federal man's voice had cracked like a bullwhip.

'I left town for a day,' Carson said. 'Met people. Asked questions. And La Lone has been seen around.'

'Whoever said that is mistaken, or lying,' Luke said hoarsely, the tin cup tight in his fists.

'I won't bother asking why anyone would do that,' Carson said. 'But why d'you suppose I let Magg and his bunch ride after you last night?'

The man's questions were dancing about like a cloud of fleas on a mangy cur, making Luke dizzy. He shook his head, looked into the fog clouding his mind, vaguely remembered complaining to Sean that Carson trusted Magg. That would explain his allowing Magg, the lawman, to ride after the fugitives. But if that was the case, why was Carson here now, at Dorado? And how had he got ahead of the posse?

'I'll make it easy for you,' Carson said, again reading his mind as he leaned over to lift the stove lid and get rid of his dead cigarette. 'I cut across country to Jake Rawlins's spread, dragged him out of bed. And he told me about the old man he saw robbing the Union Pacific.' The iron lid was replaced with a clatter. The silence built up.

'I told you,' Luke said wearily, eyes lowered to stare into his empty cup. 'Rawlins was bribed to tell a false story.'

'Not the first time, certainly not the second: when I spoke to him, I made sure he was threatened with a long spell in jail. So he told the truth.'

Something in Carson's voice brought Luke's eyes up sharply. 'And?'

'The man Rawlins saw leading that bunch of train robbers was Fess La Lone. No doubt about it: they exchanged words when La Lone came away from the railroad and led his bunch back across Rawlins's land. He threatened Rawlins. It was that threat made him lie, not a bribe. The second

173

threat — mine — made him come clean.'

'If he saw one, he saw all three.'

'Zak Theaker and Will Gall.'

'Not Magg?'

'Hell, no! He was law. But he was involved, getting a cut of the spoils.'

It was too much to swallow in one lump. Luke pushed himself out of the chair, the loose shackle banging against the wood as he placed the coffee cup on the table and crossed to the window, stared across the gallery and beyond into the distance. The sun was up over the eastern horizon. Hard-edged shadows stretched long across the yard, and the contrasting bright-ness made his eyes ache.

All he knew for sure was that nothing had been substantially changed by Carson's news. His pa and Sean were dead. If Fess La Lone had robbed the Union Pacific, he had also got Luke and Sean out of jail when they'd been falsely accused. That was the action of a good man, an honourable man. Yes, he'd kept quiet about his own involvement in the heists, but what man readily admits to guilt?

'Who killed my pa?' Luke asked without turning.

'I don't know,' Carson said.

'Why did La Lone bust us out of jail?'

'Only one possible reason: he needs you.'

'Or was it because he couldn't see us hang for a crime he committed.'

Carson shook his head. 'I don't buy that. You're seeing good in an evil man.'

And just what did that remark suggest, Luke wondered. More information Carson was keeping to himself? Or more wild conjecture?

'Well,' he said, 'you asked for talk and we've tossed some words around, but without proof what they add up to is a whole heap of nothing.'

He came away from the window, felt the room swim around him and clenched his fists until the moment passed. 'The only fact — if Rawlins is tellin' the truth — is Fess La Lone robbed some trains. I reckon Magg killed my pa, Theaker shot my brother, and Fess was trying for Magg when that slug whistled past my ear.'

'All right.' Carson tugged at his moustache, his eyes thoughtful. 'Like you, I figure Will Gall will have lit out. Made his way back to town. That leaves just the one man who can tell you if you're right or wrong. It's full daylight now. If you trust him, why don't you walk out into the yard, turn towards that ridge and flap your arms about to show your pal it's safe to come down?'

15

Luke went down the steps into the hot morning sun, took a deep breath of clean air and felt a sharp tug on the stiffness around the wound as his chest expanded. But no new warmth, no wetness. Already knitting, he decided. Painful, but clean, and without puffiness or inflamation.

Across the yard, flies buzzed in swarms around the big black horse's carcass. In front of him there was the pock-marked dust where Fess La Lone's last shot had drilled into the yard. He knew that if he stayed where he was, he was safe — and immediately marvelled at the way one man's suspicions had altered his own perceptions of an old friend.

But was it just that one man who had his doubts about La Lone? In jail, when looking for answers, he'd told Sean that the only name he could come up with was — Fess La Lone. The man's busting them out of jail had not allayed his suspicions, but simply put them to rest, and since then everything had moved too darn fast for him to do much thinking.

Carson had not planted the seeds of doubt, his common-sense arguments had been like the fresh water needed to start them sprouting. The incident at Powder River niggled; they'd been hidden from Magg's bunch when they entered the woods, yet someone had shot Sean. With a long gun. From a distance.

Now, the only man left who had any reason to kill Sean was up there on the bluff with a Sharps .50 — and again Luke found himself dizzy from thinking in circles, because their friend La Lone *had* no reason to kill Sean.

Unless he had first killed Sam Brennan.

And why, in God's name, would he do that?

Luke pursed his lips, looked at the corner of the house that cut off the outline of the bluff, the rimrock over which, once before, he'd seen Fess La Lone line up his trusty Sharps. If Luke went back on to the wide gallery and walked to the end rail, he would be exposed, but a single step would see him to safety; if he went out into the yard and La Lone was of a mind to do so, the hunter could let him walk far enough so that he was stranded in no-man's-land, with no turning back.

Goddamn!

With an irritable shake of his head, Luke walked away from the house. He stepped on the bullet mark in the dust, wriggled his boot fiercely as if to wipe away all trace of it, all memory of it, then went on until he was midway between house and bunkhouse, the barn over to his left and behind that the scrub stretching away to the bluff.

He heard a movement on the gallery, ignored it, turned to face north and, feeling like a man gone loco, waved his arms slow and wide, an army signaller who had mislaid his flags. Something inside him tightened. Suddenly, his mouth was dry. It was as if Carson's suspicions were expanding within him, screaming truth. He saw his father's body, the bloody slashes and the grey, whiskery face, and for the first time since talking to the hunter he thought of the man's skinning knives — went beyond that to recall the men in the barn and the absence of blood on any of them; the sounds, his suspicion at the time that there was someone else there, up in the hay-loft —

Far away, high up on the rimrock, sunlight flashed mirror-like on polished metal. From the gallery, Carson roared a warning. Luke spun, felt his back prickle as he ran for the gallery, heard the roar of the shot and the whine of a bullet cutting the air behind him.

He hit the steps, took them in two long strides, marvelling as he did so that the sounds had come out of sequence: he'd heard La Lone's shot, then the flight of the bullet. But as he crossed the gallery towards the door and Carson came from the side rails to meet him, he saw why: the marshal was carrying Sam Brennan's Hunsicker Long Rifle; it was his shot Luke had heard as the federal man spotted that flash of sunlight on the barrel of La Lone's Sharps, and used the venerable weapon to drive the hunter back off the rimrock.

'The warning saved my life,' Luke said. 'But what about that shot?'

Carson pulled a face. 'Close enough to make him sweat, no more.'

A rivulet of sweat crawled down Luke's cheek. He reached out, took the long rifle from Carson, turned it in his hands so that the rich, polished stock caught the sunlight.

'Magg used this,' he said softly. 'Or Theaker. When Sean was dyin' up there, one of them was drilling shots into that rimrock.'

'And now it's up to me and you,' Carson said. 'Or are you still of a mind to give that devil the benefit of the doubt?'

'I could think of a number of reasons why I should,' Luke said, and saw Carson roll his eyes in despair. 'But some time back, I asked myself a question, then got kinda lost. Maybe you can come up with the answer.'

'Try me.'

'Why is he up on that bluff? What's he doin' there?'

'Could be he saw me coming when I rode in — but seein' as I arrived before him, that's out.' Carson smiled crookedly. 'Another question you might ask is, if I came here from talking to Rawlins and knew La Lone had led those train robbers, why didn't I arrest him?'

'Go on.'

'He rode straight on through, and that puzzled me. I know the trail he took; I followed it when you boys were having trouble with Magg, and it goes nowhere, peters out beyond that bluff.'

'Which brings us back full circle:

why's he up there?'

'Because that's where he hid the cash.'

The boards creaked as Luke shifted his weight. The sun was higher now, the gallery in deep shade but as hot as a Dutch oven. His palm was damp on the Hunsicker, and he changed his grip and wiped his free hand on his pants.

He knew Carson was wrong, had to be. Fess La Lone had sweated blood with them as they hunted through tangled mesquite for that cash; no man who already had it safely stashed away would have wasted such time and effort. Even if the unthinkable, the unpalatable, turned out to be the truth, every way Luke turned there were contradictions. If La Lone knew the stolen money was on the bluff, then Luke could understand why he'd wanted to remain there when he and Sean walked down to Cleaver Magg. But the hunter would then have lit out with the money. Instead, he'd followed them to Linch, and shadowed the hunt as Luke and Sean made their second escape. And still he was here, blasting away with the Sharps.

'Let's go inside,' Luke said.

The coffee was still hot on the stove. He propped the long rifle against the table, poured two drinks and handed one to Carson. The marshal tasted it, pulled a face. He cocked an eyebrow at Luke.

'You figure I'm wrong?'

'I do. I mean, if he had it, why the hell didn't he ride out when we left that bluff — and why's he still here?'

'I don't know — but I've got a good idea, and if I'm right I — '

'Rider coming!'

★ ★ ★

Luke slammed the cup on the table, swept up the rifle and ran for the door. As he did so the horseman came hammering down into the yard drawing a cloud of dust like a dun curtain across the dazzling sunlight. He raced past, close to the bunkhouse. From the log walls, a sliver of timber flew into the air, exposing white wood. The thud of the big Sharps followed, but now the rider was down the slope and, as Luke raced along the gallery, he saw him slowing in the shelter of the barn, then moving his horse at an easy trot towards the trail that led around the acres of scrub.

'Will Gall,' he shouted. 'He's ridin' my horse, maybe — '

'Get back!'

The bullet drilled into the upright alongside Luke's head. He stepped back against the wall, flashed a grimace at Carson.

'Will I ever get the hang of this?'

'Every man has his special skills,' Carson said.

'Like I was about to say,' Luke said, 'maybe Gall's the reason why La Lone's been hangin' around.'

'So let's go find out.'

'But not with this.'

Carson looked at Sam Brennan's Hunsicker, and shook his head.

'No. Any fighting done'll be close range, you'll need one of your pa's pistols.'

In the rack against the wall there were the rifles Magg and Theaker had left untouched, his pa's gun-belt hanging on a peg. He unbuckled his own belt, strapped on his pa's and settled it. When he turned to Carson, the marshal was nodding approval.

'Remington .44. Your pa chose well.'

'Did him no damn good, in the end,' Luke said. 'You ready?'

'When you are.'

All right. Let's go get this settled.'

16

They rode double, Luke tight up behind Carson, the Deputy US Marshal mostly using his knees to guide the horse along the flank of the high, timbered slope as, against his own advice, he cradled a Winchester across his thighs and his narrowed eyes tried to look in four directions at the same time.

They had moved fast, running around the blind side of the house to the barn where Carson had left his horse, then taking the same trail followed by Gall. Along it, acrid dust still hung in the hot air. From not too far ahead they could hear the faint sounds of Gall's progress.

Would they be audible to La Lone? Once a rider passed beyond the barn, he would be out of sight to a watcher up on the bluff. There had been no more shots, and Luke could imagine the hunter sweating, turning uneasily away from the rimrock to face the trees. If an attack came from that direction, he would be caught with his pants down — and the only way up or down was through the timber.

'Seems to me,' Carson said, 'to reach that rimrock we need to double back.'

'Yeah, up through the trees a-ways till we reach some open ground. La Lone stays there, he's exposed. I think he'll move, come down to join Will Gall.'

'No doubt you're right — but what I'm thinking is, when Gall turns back on himself and rides up the slope, he looks down he's likely to catch sight of us.'

Even as he spoke, a rifle cracked almost above their heads. The impact registered as the solid, meaty smack of lead on flesh-covered bone. Without a sound, the horse stumbled and went down. Luke rolled clear, wriggled behind a grassy bank and went still. Carson was unlucky. He hit the ground hard, tried to pull clear and his foot got tangled in a stirrup leather. The horse flopped slackly, its dead weight pinning his leg to the ground. Flat on his back, he planted his other foot on the saddle, braced himself and pushed. Then another shot cracked. Dirt spurted alongside his head. Abandoning the attempt to get free he twisted awkwardly to lift himself up on one elbow, flipped out his sixgun and blasted three fast shots at the trees.

The blast of gunpowder was ringing in Luke's ears, the hot stink of it in his nostrils as he came away from the bank and dropped alongside the marshal. He grabbed the trapped leg, planted both feet against the horse and pulled. As the rifle went silent, Carson renewed his efforts, face tight as he struggled against the dead weight pinning him to the ground.

The rifle cracked again. The marshal grunted, dropped his sixgun as if he'd caught hold of the wrong end of a hot running-iron, and went limp. As he did so, his leg abruptly slid free, slipping as easily out of his boot as if slathered in axle-grease. With a quick swoop, Luke grabbed the marshal's pistol, sprang to his feet and sprayed the timber with slugs from both sixguns. He was rewarded with a sharp yelp of pain. The rifle went silent. Twigs snapped as Will Gall retreated.

'Flesh wound,' Carson said through his teeth. Blood trickled between his fingers as his left hand clasped his right forearm. He rolled on to his knees, climbed to his feet.

'He's made damn sure we're on foot,' Luke said, 'but that don't matter. In those trees, a horse'd only get in the way.'

'But if him and La Lone make a run for it, we're left flat-footed.'

'No.' Luke shook his head. 'There's only one way up or down.'

Carson grinned. 'So we've got 'em both pinned down?'

'I have — unless you can shoot left-handed.'

'Hell, I reckon we're going to get so close I'd have to struggle to miss.'

'Here,' Luke said, 'let's strap that arm.'

That quickly done, they scrambled up the side of the slope and soundlessly entered the trees. The tang of gun-smoke was in the air. As they stood still and listened, the weighted silence was like the intense quiet preceding a storm.

'Those two have got more than they bargained for,' Carson said softly.

'La Lone knew there's only the one way down, knew there was a chance he'd be trapped,' Luke said. 'Why come up here?'

'That's easy,' Carson said. 'He couldn't carry the cash with him when he followed you to Linch, picked off Sean, and the others — so he's come back for it. As for the rest, why he waited around . . . ' In the dappled sunlight his face was a mask, his eyes unreadable. 'This business is still troubling you. You think I'm wrong

191

about the money.' A statement — and still he watched Luke.

'I don't know what I think,' Luke said, 'but I know there's no time.'

He left Carson and cut across the slope, found the tracks made by Will Gall's horse and turned uphill. He climbed awkwardly, recalling carrying Sean that same way and marvelled at his own strength.

Carson caught up with him, panting. Fifty yards ahead, the edge of the trees was marked by bright sunlight. Before they'd gone twenty-five, Will Gall's rifle opened up and they dropped and flattened themselves to the ground as bullets snicked through the trees. The Winchester hammered away, loosed a full magazine, then fell silent.

'That was from about as far back as he can get,' Carson said, and spat out a fragment of leaf. 'I reckon he's joined up with La Lone. We're in for a fight.'

'Trouble is, we didn't make the edge of the trees and they got the jump on us. All they need do now is set back and wait. The minute we walk out . . . '

'Depends *where* we walk out,' said Carson.

Luke nodded doubtfully. 'Difficult to outflank them. But something's got to be done. I've got a good right arm. You stay here, let go the occasional shot to keep them interested. I'll try to make my way around. When you hear shooting . . . '

He saw the marshal nod, tight-lipped, touched his shoulder, then rolled away, came up into a crouch and started across the slope. There was an oily click, and Carson's pistol cracked. Gall's rifle answered, the bullet whispering wickedly through the trees behind Luke as he moved away.

They had been skirting the western side of the bluff when Gall opened fire from above and killed Carson's horse; when he retreated they had doubled back on themselves to move uphill through the trees. Luke was now working his way east. After fifty yards he figured he'd gone far enough, turned right, and began pushing up the slope.

Again Carson's pistol cracked. Again it was answered by Gall's rifle. La Lone's Sharps remained silent — and Luke felt a worm of unease stir. What were they playing at? Where was La Lone?

He pushed on, looking up towards the sunlight and anxiously listening, skirted a massive, moss-covered boulder that at some time in the distant past had broken loose from the rim and rolled down the slope into the trees — and stumbled into a recently dug hole.

He went heavily to his knees, cracked an elbow against the rock and swore softly. But his eyes were busy, his mind racing. The hole was shallow. At the bottom there was a bulky burlap sack, half buried, caked in damp soil. Stencilled lettering revealed as he brushed away the dirt told Luke it was the property of the Union Pacific. When he opened the sack and thrust his hand inside he found it packed with banknotes in thick bundles.

As he rocked back on to his heels he recalled how, with Magg and Theaker at the barn and Lannigan and Gall waiting down at the foot of the slope, Fess La Lone had left his Sharps up on the rimrock and walked down into these woods. He had spent some time there, and returned to Luke and Sean with a look on his face that, at the time, Luke couldn't read. Now, he knew that it had been triumph: La Lone had bust a gut trying to find the money down in the scrub, then walked into the woods and stumbled on it by accident.

Luke dragged the sack out of the dirt, carried it twenty yards deeper into the woods, gathered brushwood and covered it over. He did it with amusement tainted with bitterness: he had buried a deer, buried his brother, and now he'd buried a sack of cash, and two out of the three bore the scars of a knife he had wielded.

There was some puzzlement as he straightened and stepped back to admire his handiwork: if La Lone was the brains behind the train robberies, who had hidden the money on the bluff? And again the sharp blade of the big Bowie knife surfaced to provide an answer that was so clear, so obvious, and led to other conclusions so chilling, that it took Luke Brennan's breath away.

★   ★   ★

The bluff sloped down from south to north, a giant wedge of land with the sheer face at its blunt end facing Dorado. At the top it fell away steeply to each side in smooth, rounded grassy slopes; lower down, those slopes were more gradual, and tree-covered. When Luke emerged from the woods he was dangerously close to the rimrock, but hidden from La Lone's position by the bluff's contours.

The sun was directly overhead, beating down. Vaguely aware that Carson's pistol had been silent for some time, much more conscious of the gut-feeling of uneasiness that was screaming at him that something was wrong, he started up the slope.

Underfoot, the crisp glass was slippery; more than once a foot went from under him and he went down on all fours. By this time, too, his breath was hissing through pinched nostrils, salt sweat running into his eyes. Lightheadness was still troubling him, and from time to time he squeezed his eyes tight shut until the giddiness passed.

He made his way sideways as well as up, and in this fashion reached the rimrock downslope from La Lone and looked out across the stretch of scrub to Dorado. Here, he took a breather, and was standing spread-legged with hands on hips when a fusillade of shots rang out from the woods.

Instinctively, he turned towards the sound, head cocked to listen. Pistols, this time, in a rapid exchange of shots, and Luke cursed softly as he pictured Carson facing a surprise attack with his .45 held in the wrong hand. Just as

Carson's pistol had been used to fool Fess La Lone into believing they were pinned down in the woods, so Will Gall's Winchester had been used to convince the US marshal that the two men were still up on the rimrock. But one of them had moved — Luke guessed it would be the big deputy, Will Gall — and, under cover of the rifle fire from La Lone, had slipped across the open ground and into the woods.

That left La Lone on the rimrock. He was a crack shot with the Sharps, chillingly adept with a knife — Luke's jaw muscles bunched painfully at the thought — but nigh on useless with a pistol. If he was staring in the direction of the gunfire — still snapping like a string of firecrackers — then now was the time to move.

Yet even as he turned away from the sounds of the battle, he saw that he was too late: ten yards away, outlined against the brassy sun, Fess La Lone was looking down on him along the barrel of the Sharps. His narrowed blue eyes were like slivers of wet stone. His finger was white on the trigger.

★ ★ ★

'Knives are more your style,' Luke said.

La Lone sneered. 'Any way you want it,' he said.

'Like Pa?'

'Your pa was happy to have us use his house, for a stiff price. Your wire knocked him sideways. Seems he couldn't face you and Sean with all that thieving going on, and him in the thick of it.'

'So he took the money, hid it?' Luke read the answer in the little hunter's eyes, knew that his father's double-cross to protect his sons from the sight of his aberration had provoked a ferocious reaction.

'You were there,' he said, his eyes on the man's trigger finger. 'Up in the loft. There was no blood on Magg, or the others. And they were gunmen, of a sort, not artists with a skinning knife.'

'Sam held out to the end, died before he'd talk. After that, I knew I needed you. You and Sean were brought up on Dorado. I figured if your pa hid the money, you'd know where.' He eased the Sharps, spat into the grass. 'So I bust you out of jail, brought you out here only to find you knew less than me.'

'Then you stumbled on it.'

La Lone chuckled. 'Yeah, ain't that a laugh? And once I had it I didn't need you, didn't need the others, and they were so occupied chasing you and Sean halfway across Wyoming Territory, they were sitting ducks.'

'So why wait around?'

'Because I know you, Luke Brennan. I killed your pa, and your brother. Better to get you out of my hair now, than spend the rest of my life looking over my shoulder.'

Maybe there was some feeling left, a trace of regret for the killing that had been sparked by a son's telegraph message to his proud father. With those final words, La Lone's eyes had clouded. For an instant, he was not seeing Luke as he stood before him, but the boy he had known; perhaps, too, seeing again the mute accusation in an old man's eyes as he stoically bore the agony of the skinning knives; eyes that La Lone would take with him to the grave.

And it was in that instant that Luke ducked low and went for his sixgun; saw the blue eyes snap and the Sharps dip and the trigger-finger whiten and knew, again, that he'd misjudged and was about to die.

The first shot was a vicious crack — but from another direction. Another followed, then Luke was lunging sideways, floating, pistol out and spitting, dropping lazily towards the wiry grass as reality was suspended and the moments stretched to eternity, then hitting solid earth with a jarring thump that told him he was alive.

The thud of the big Sharps was a solid impact on eardrums, the gout of earth that kicked dirt into his face testimony to the waywardness of the shot. For, even as he squeezed the trigger, Fess La Lone was being blown backwards. His startled eyes had flicked left as Tom Carson burst from the woods with sixgun wildly blazing and bullets whistled close to his head. Those same eyes suddenly dilated in shocked disbelief as slugs from Sam Brennan's Remington .44 punched into his chest with an accuracy that Luke Brennan, a moderately bad shot, was to recall with wonder at odd moments throughout the rest of his life.

Then the hunter was gone, falling lifeless from the jagged rimrock in an aching silence that was followed, from far below, by the faint crackle of chaparral.

Fess La Lone was dead.

Luke had reached the end of a long and bloody trail.